//
British
Marine Engineer

Liana Margiva

British Marine Engineer

Copyright © 2023 by Liana Margiva

Paperback ISBN: 978-1-63812-564-8
Ebook ISBN: 978-1-63812-565-5
Hardcover ISBN: 978-1-63812-910-3

All rights reserved. No part in this book may be produced and transmitted in any form or by any means, electronic, or mechanical, including photocopying, recording, or by any information storage and retrieval system, without permission in writing from the copyright owner.

The views expressed in this work are solely those of the author and do not necessarily reflect the views of the publisher hereby disclaims any responsibility for them.

Published by Pen Culture Solutions 01/23/2023

Pen Culture Solutions
1-888-727-7204 (USA)
1-800-950-458 (Australia)
support@penculturesolutions.com

ABOUT PROSE AND POETRY OF LIANA MARGIVA

It is a privilege and honor to appreciate your creative works. "Sleepless Nights" is a touching story.

I am impr essed with the writing style of Author Liana Margiva and also with the translation by Anatol Kardiukov, which showed the artistic vein of both creative Masters. I have enjoyed the reading/The Vincent Island/

You write with a beautiful and enjoyable style. / Strange Woman/

Every time I read your work, I learn and educate my writing tools. This composition is a glowing page of short story that inspires and enchant the reader. "The Witch" has filled a new chapter on the history of short story. I salute you, Author-Poet Liana Margiva. May Your pen never! You write with a beautiful and enjoyable style.

Andre Bendavi ben -Yehu

This work is a composition that does lend a golden chapter to the history of short stories; and reveal to the reader how a profound and artistic Author honor his/her are and language. "The Witch" I read and am satisfied and intellectually fed.

Margarita Caligaris

You are a magnificent story teller! This work is superb!/Sleepless Nights/ Very well written with the heart of one who knows and has written and received such Letters. /Letters/ Exceptional and a keeper! Your phrases are hauntingly and so sad, beautiful./Strange Woman/ A marvelous nostalgic work of a melancholy one who is alone and feels the emptiness of loves lost./Moon, why you hide behind the clouds/

JMS BELL

A soul laid bare in love and its longing. Beautifully rendered with the moon and stars as backdrop./Moon why you hide behind the clouds/ Love is such a fickle thing, you have described it so well here, with all its ups and downs, its fire and it falsity, and in the end what is the love but the true love of God. Excellent work. / Friend/ A grim reminder of the realities that we now see around us during this Great Pandemic. A finely written poem on death that we must all reckon with in own way./Death/

John Herlihy

A moving tapestry of thoughts. /Death/

Richard Cederberg

Very touching! What an excellent Teller you are! With gifts so rare that you share so passionately./ Sleepless Nights/ This is a very powerfully written sad story. What a wonderful gift you have. May God continually bless the work of your hands. /The Vincent Island/

Margaret Christine Mullings

Your writing style, as always, incredible! /Strange Woman/ This is wonderful. You are such a gifted Writer. /The Witch/

Dawn Anderson

Superb writing-splendid! /Sleepless Nights/ Bravo on this exceptionally penned story-loved it! /The Witch/

A Serviceable Villain

Brilliant work… just splendid. /Sleepless Nights/

Vesna Petkovic

Such a passionate expression of unrequited love! / Moon, why you hide behind the clouds/

Regis Auffray

This is sad, but it feels like legend. Great work telling this tale. /The Vincent Island/

Sheila Roy

I must say "a truly wonderful story."/The Witch/

William Butler

Liana, this is a great story, really well done. It's an interesting tale, and told and developed really well. /The Witch/

Angel Editing

Wow, an awesome story. /The Witch/

M. Teresa Clayton

Written with passion and with a style that shows me that this Author is capable of much greater things. /The Witch/

Gerald Tate

"The Witch" is very well written and constructed.
Gwendolyn Thomas Gath

You had me captivated from the first word to the last! /The Witch/

Christine Tsen

I enjoyed this story very much. /The Witch/

Tommy Thomas

A great story. It held my interest completely. /The Witch/

Mary Patterson

Dedicated to Fatih

THE BRITISH MARINE ENGINEER

Lorena was far away from home. One of her friends was going out of town and had asked Lorena to babysit her mother for the duration of her trip.

The eighty-year old was, despite her age, still a vigorous woman and could take care of herself, but her daughter was reluctant to leave her on her own. Lorena couldn't say no since she lived by herself and, at the time, was not working. She quickly packed and moved to her friend's house.

The woman turned out to be a quiet person, not senile in any way. All day long she either watched TV or snoozed in her vintage recliner. Lorena's new abode was on a busy street, which constantly manifested its presence with the incessant hum of rushing traffic. The neighborhood was a canine heaven. A white colonial on one side was home to four furry mutts that the owner walked several times a day. Whenever the dogs spotted Lorena outside the house, they burst out barking and growling menacingly, determined to rip the stranger to shreds. The only obstacle preventing them from completing their macabre mission was a tall chain-link fence that separated the properties. On the other side lived a large red beast prone to nocturnal oratories, announcing each and every passerby with demonic howling and barking. The old woman's house was flanked on both sides by tall trees, their bare branches studded with flocks of birds that, eager for spring warmth and lush summer foliage, entertained the neighborhood with dismal chirping. Beyond the trees Lorena could make out decrepit greenhouses where neighbors used to grow flowers.

The old woman's house, an old two-story colonial that knew better days, featured a tall glass front door—the only decoration and the centerpiece of the otherwise drab facade.

All day long Lorena watched TV with the old woman, both of them sharing a passion for old Westerns. The woman relaxed in her recliner, Lorena next to her on an overstuffed chair. The living-room window overlooked a small front yard and the street beyond where a traffic light blinked incessantly, driving Lorena insane, so she had to close her eyes during commercials.

The old woman's bedroom, which adjoined the living room, featured a twin-size bed and a vintage TV. Lorena's bedroom upstairs was crammed with the old woman's possessions. The only window, just like the one in the living room, looked out onto the street with its wretched traffic light blinking straight into Lorena's eyes when she raised her head from her pillow.

During the day Lorena ventured into the unkempt front yard to get a breath of fresh air. Shortly after she moved in, Lorena looked out into the yard through the glass door, feeling miserable and having second thoughts about her decision. *This is, indeed, a cage*, she thought, but there was no backing out. Lorena was good-natured, joyful, and had a good sense of humor, which helped her through many of the hardships that had befallen her. However, in the deepest crevasses of her soul lurked other feelings, thoroughly suppressed and shielded behind a seemingly impenetrable wall of vitality and banter. Lorena's entire personality projected an air of exhilaration, convincing the uninitiated that she was the happiest creature on Earth, for no unhappy human being could possibly be so playful and giggly.

Yet, sequestered at the bottom of Laura's soul lingered a dark stigma of loneliness. She had no choice but to subdue this feeling. After all, there was nothing she could do about it, so why bother digging it out? God only knew what else might be lurking in those depths.

Within days, Lorena got sick of watching TV, her nature screaming for change. She put a photograph of herself posing with a bouquet of yellow flowers on a website where people posted their pictures and poets their verse. When the old woman dozed off, Lorena picked up her phone, read amateur poetry, and checked out the photos. Feeling reconnected to humanity, she cheered up.

On Saturday the old woman's relatives took her away for a day, leaving Lorena alone in the house. That evening Lorena sat in the kitchen, reading the latest posts on the website. Suddenly, a message popped up on the screen, featuring a small, round photo of a gray-haired man in a light-blue shirt. The picture was tiny but large enough for Lorena to see the man looked very pleasant. The stranger greeted Lorena, asking if he was interrupting something. The message appeared out of the blue, and although Lorena felt confused for a moment, she managed to respond. The man in the photograph introduced himself as Douglas. He was from Great Britain. Lorena instantly felt a certain deference for the stranger, the feeling she always associated with that country and its cultural heritage. Douglas was a marine engineer who worked under contract near the Atlantic Ocean—in fact, in the ocean. At his location, it was late at night, but he was unable to sleep. He was sixty, had been widowed for four years, and had a seven-year-old son, a late child, who was at boarding school. Every message from Douglas was accompanied by the same photo, making the dialogue very personal.

Lorena felt strangely comfortable conversing with Douglas, and he seemed to be equally relaxed, as if they had known each other for years. She was so absorbed in the conversation that she lost track of time and was brought back to reality only when the old woman returned to the house. Lorena typed a quick goodbye, and Douglas promised to get in touch the following day.

Chatting with the stranger gave Lorena a sense of elation, relief, a welcome break from her daily routine. She felt strangely attracted to Douglas, a feeling enhanced by his photograph popping up next to every text message, his smiling countenance making the man very likable. Lorena felt strangely special from the beginning of their discourse, whether it was Douglas' Britishness, which invoked the greatness of the nation, or the fact that it had been over twelve years since she had had any emotional contact with a man. Lorena's heart opened to Douglas instantly, his amiable smile on a small photograph projecting the goodness of his nature.

The next morning Lorena awoke to a fresh message from Douglas. He was grateful for their conversation and her willingness to make friends. He also mentioned that he felt lonely and miserable. Lorena felt instant empathy for the Brit and asked him to tell her more about himself. He told her about mourning his late spouse and his profound love for his seven-year-old son. Lorena concluded that Douglas was a very decent human being as he was still harboring such pain four years after his wife's demise.

Douglas never talked much about his work, though he sent one photograph depicting a platform on long steel legs towering over the ocean. Men in orange jumpsuits fussed around some equipment being unloaded from a large helicopter. Another man in an orange jumpsuit posed for the photograph. Although she couldn't make out his face, Lorena realized it was Douglas. He casually mentioned his recent descent into ocean depths, invoking instant awe in Lorena.

She closed her eyes, visualizing Douglas descending into the ocean burdened with dive gear and instruments while Lorena approached him, wearing flippers and goggles, like a modern-day mermaid. Douglas became aware of Lorena's presence but failed to recognize her. She touched his hand gently, and his face lit up with the same amiable smile from the photograph. He nodded, took Lorena by the hand, and guided her through the turquoise water. Fish of all shapes and sizes milled about, basking in faint sunlight. They were surrounded by total silence and unparalleled beauty.

A while later, Douglas released her hand, waved, and then continued his descent into blue murkiness while Lorena swam toward the surface. She opened her eyes reluctantly. Oh, if only she could live close to the ocean, breathe its salty freshness, and listen to the surf's lullaby! She would never, ever feel lonely again. The ocean would fill her soul, leaving no place for dark feelings to hide.

Two days later, Douglas called Lorena his best friend ever. His words touched her deeply. She sat staring into the front yard through the glass door, thinking of Douglas. Little did she know then that she would never be able to shut him out of her soul, that he would always be beside her, in her dreams. The cage she was confined to, albeit temporarily, hardly brought Lorena any joy, but it couldn't prevent her from being carried away in her dreams to the ocean beach next to Douglas. They were on the sand, side by side, Lorena's eyes fixated on Douglas's smiling face. Unable to speak, mesmerized by his presence, Lorena longed to touch his cheek, caress his face, but she resisted the urge. After a while, feeling emboldened, she spoke in a low voice. "May I touch your face?"

Douglas kept on staring at her, smiling smartly, as if knowing what was happening in Lorena's soul.

"Certainly," he whispered and smiled again.

Lorena reached out slowly and then ran her shaky fingers across his cheek. Douglas kept smiling, then took Lorena by the hand and looked straight into her eyes. He reached out and touched Lorena's cheek, then leaned over and gently kissed her lips. Lorena closed her eyes. She wanted to save this memory, to savor it, to allow it to warm her soul when she became lonely once again.

Douglas continued writing to her diligently every morning and night, occasionally dropping a line in the middle of the day. Every morning Lorena woke up to a message filled with that tenderest words that would make any poet green with envy.

Joy came to Lorena's life, lit up her face with a smile, and filled her soul with peace. She fell in love with Douglas, filled the deepest nooks of her heart with him. She craved his letters and thought about him almost every minute. It had taken a British marine engineer to rekindle the smoldering embers of Lorena's passion. She couldn't help but wonder how a man whom she had never met could set her soul on fire.

Soon Douglas stopped calling Lorena his best friend and told her he was in love with her. He missed the warmth of a woman's embrace and longed for eyes filled with desire. In the cold, lonely depths of Atlantic ocean, he was thinking of Lorena, warming his heart with his imaginary love.

Soon, Douglas sent her two large portraits of himself. They were from his office in London, he explained. "My God, isn't he handsome!" Lorena exclaimed when she saw the photos. Having said that, she realized Douglas's appearance was no longer an issue. For all she cared, he could be the most ordinary person. She had fallen in love with the beauty of his soul, sensitive and romantic, harbored in the body of this sixty-year old marine engineer. His handsome, pleasant face with light-hazel eyes radiated kindness. Lorena stared at Douglas's smiling countenance, feeling her heart swell with love. Gently, as if being careful not to hurt him, Lorena ran her finger across his face on the screen, almost feeling the warmth of his skin. His kind smile with slightly parted lips invoked a desire to touch them.

Lorena closed her eyes, so nothing could stand in the way of her dream, which carried her to the distant beach. Douglas was lying on the sand, his eyes closed, resting after a day of hard work. Lorena approached him and touched his shoulder.

"Douglas," she said in a low voice.

"You've come. I was waiting, I was so looking forward to see you!" he said, breaking into a smile. Lorena lay down beside him, snuggled closer, placed her head on his chest, put her arm around him, and then froze. The ocean watched them keenly, kicked up small waves, frolicking, then playfully threw a larger wave on the beach, splashing the two with salty water. They jumped to their feet, standing close to each other as if their bodies were one. Douglas peered silently at Lorena with his trademark smile. She reached up and touched his face, stroked his forehead, and looked him in the eye. Douglas kept smiling blissfully. The gentle touch of her trembling fingers said more than any words. Lorena smiled back, wishing to say something, but failed.

"I know, I know," Douglas said, wrapping his arm around Lorena's waist, "your hand has just told me."

Day after day, several times a day, Douglas wrote messages to Lorena, astounding her with an avalanche of affection. Little did he know that the men Lorena used to love never responded in kind, intimidated by her exuberant passion. This time, a lonely marine engineer stuck in the middle of the ocean had fallen in love with Lorena. But were his feelings true? Many would question the sincerity of Douglas's emotions, but not Lorena, who fell hopelessly in love with the warmth and sensitivity projected by Douglas's personality, with the affection that erupted from his lonely heart and swept Lorena off her feet.

She kept scrutinizing Douglas's photographs, looking for answers, finding nothing but affirmation of his feelings in his kind, affectionate gaze. Lorena studied Douglas's photographs so well, every detail of his face etched firmly in her memory, so visualizing him was easy.

She responded to Douglas's love messages with passion, telling him she was madly in love and would keep loving him as long as she lived. Douglas was unaware that Lorena's passion sprang out of her love-hungry heart, which had never known the bliss of reciprocal affection. The love that Lorena had dreamed of her entire life, the one she was longing for like a desert wanderer yearned for water, remained as distant as ever, fading slowly into obscurity. Lorena had long abandoned her lifelong search, fearing that her heart couldn't take any more of the misery and pain that love had inflicted upon her. Then, like a bolt from the blue, the British marine engineer had entered, drowning Lorena in his affection, bringing her heart out of protracted hibernation, and releasing a roaring inferno of passion that overshadowed any and all previous flareups. Lorena fell in love with Douglas with the fervor of a woman who had her beloved within arm's reach, not a thousand miles away in the middle of nowhere.

Good morning to you, my beautiful Lorena, the most stunning woman in the whole world! My darling, I am praising the Lord for our relationship, hoping that you'll remain in my life forever. Like a magic key, your words unlocked my heart. I never imagined that I was capable of loving someone like I love you. I swear to keep you in my soul eternally and to never break your heart. Your presence in my life gives me a reason to carry on and a hope for joy that I haven't felt for many years. I wish I had met you years ago. The thought of years lost without you makes me miserable. I adore your kind heart, the way you differ from many. For the first time in my rather long life I have found love in someone's heart, and I promise to love you as long as my heart keeps beating. Knowing you would make any man blissful, and I thank God for granting me this precious gift.

When reading messages from Douglas, Lorena often imagined herself beside him on the beach, touching his hand, stroking his shoulder, looking him in the eyes. Douglas would lean over, tenderly touching her lips with his. Lorena would respond to his kiss with equal tenderness, albeit with greater passion since only someone who had never experienced the joy of mutual affection was capable of such strong emotions.

"I love you, sweetheart," Douglas would say. Lorena embraced him, her eyes filling with tears of joy and gratitude. She felt loved.

With each passing day, Lorena fell more and more in love with Douglas. She used to commiserate with the pain in his words when he wrote about his late wife, but now, although Douglas never mentioned her again, the thought annoyed Lorena. The possibility that her beloved marine engineer could be intimate with someone else, even his lawfully wedded wife, drove Lorena insane. She was too deeply in love with Douglas to share him with anyone! Every time she thought about it, Lorena felt so adamant that she had a hard time dealing with it. Not that Lorena had never had relationships in the past; she just couldn't deal with the idea that Douglas may have been close to another woman. His amiable gaze and his cordial smile couldn't possibly belong to anyone but Lorena, who, nevertheless, was fully aware that the man couldn't have just sit on the beach till his sixties, waiting for her. She never grew tired of looking at his picture, which stoked her joy every time she brought it on her phone screen. Lorena would look at it before going to bed and fall asleep with a smile on her face. When she opened her eyes in the morning she'd look at it again to give her day a happy kickstart.

However, as time went by, Douglas's photo began to cause mixed feelings. Alongside joy, something else crept into her soul: fear. The thought of losing Douglas began to poison her mind and made her eyes cloud with tears.

Good morning, darling Lorena! My heart fills with joy when I think about you. I will be forever indebted to you for the light you brought into my life. For the happiness you have filled my dreary existence with, please take my heart and my love. I am with you wherever I am and in your heart as well. You are the joy of my life, a delight that makes my day. I wish your heart to be filled with joy and love every moment of every day. This is what I want you to know: I love you much, much more than you could ever love me. So, here's my heart. Take it; it belongs to no one else but you till the moment it stops beating. On this bright spring day, may the sun shine upon you, warming you with my love!

Lorena was so profoundly touched by Douglas's words that it took her a while to come to her senses. Sitting beside the old woman in front of the TV, she often closed her eyes, visualizing Douglas next to her, taking her hand in his. She could almost feel the warmth of his hand. It went straight to Lorena's heart, soothing it. Her life no longer seemed purposeless and bleak the way it was before she met Douglas. She looked forward to every morning, which brought with it a new letter filled with love and admiration. The soul of the gray-haired British marine engineer with a kind smile harbored enough romanticism to make his fellow Englishman Shakespeare pale in comparison. After reading Douglas's letters, the great bard would certainly lose sleep for a while.

Perhaps Douglas would love Lorena less or wouldn't have fallen for her at all had he been in London among multitudes of his compatriots. Now, being away from it all in an all-male environment and in the middle of the ocean to boot, descending into the dark, lonesome abyss, his heart was longing for love, the warmth of a woman's embrace, and tender touches. The volcano in his soul had finally awakened, sending a pyroclastic flow of unspent affection toward Lorena. Rereading countless letters from Douglas, Lorena was stunned by the extent of romanticism, warmth, and affection that emanated from the man's soul.

Whimpering over the heart-wrenching "Letter From an Unknown Woman" by Stefan Zweig, women tended to assume that only a woman's soul could harbor romanticism and affection, ignoring the fact that the author of the most fascinating love letter was, in fact, a man. Women were also oblivious to the fact that it was male writers who broke many a woman's heart by their timeless romance novels. Women stubbornly continued claiming exclusive proprietorship over romance. Those women deserved a reprieve, for they had never met anyone like Douglas and thus couldn't possibly fathom boundless affection and a thirst for love sizzling in the soul of a British marine engineer. The letters from Douglas were as romantic as Stefan Zweig's, but what was really amazing was that they were addressed to Lorena.

Douglas wrote that he had spoken to his son about Lorena, telling him he had found the boy a new mother. Douglas said the boy was delighted and asked his father to say hello to Lorena. She was profoundly moved and, although tears never came, felt her heart was weeping. Lorena had grown up without a mother and could easily understand little boy's feelings. That day Douglas wrote Lorena another letter, which had a bombshell effect on her.

My darling Lorena, when I think about love, the first thing that comes to mind is you. Love is an amazing feeling. You are the best thing that has happened to me in my lifetime. My son is asking me to call him every day and send you greetings and love from both of us. Trust me, dear, I will do my darndest to make you happier with each passing day, week, and year. I love you, and I will continue to love you till the day I die. My son also has the grandest feelings for you. Imagine that! You are now so deeply rooted in my heart and mind that you'll remain there forever. I am so looking forward to meeting you, being with you, going together through whatever lies ahead of us. I miss you more and more with each passing day. Entrust your heart to me, consider me your destiny, and I will be true to you till the end of days. I only beg for one thing: please, don't wound my heart, for this time it will be a mortal wound. Lorena, I want you to know that all I am wishing for on this Earth is you, my love!

Having read the letter, Lorena was bitter since he had mentioned this several times in his previous writing. Someone must have hurt him deeply, but Lorena was reluctant to query Douglas about it. She immediately sat down and wrote a response.

Dearest Douglas,

I already wrote to you that it has been over twelve years since I stopped looking for love. I even forgot it existed, for I failed to find it. All those years I shunned the subject, being fully aware that my heart couldn't get over any more deception and cheating. I wish you knew how many times a day I look at your photograph! It is the only joy in my life. Every time I see your face, I know it will be in my heart forever. That's why I asked you for more photos.

Douglas didn't wait long to respond.

I am crazy about you. Meeting you wasn't an accident. The timing was exactly right. You are and will always be in my heart.

Lorena was lost for words. She had a hard time believing that someone who knew her only by an electronic image and a few letters could have fallen so madly in love with her, a woman stuck in perpetual solitude and rejected by love. Lorena tried to ignore the logic that a mature man who had known a happy family life was capable of true love. She chased away the thought that perhaps the romantic soul of a man unplugged from civilization and craving female attention in the middle of the Atlantic had created an idol, embellishing it with qualities that she wouldn't be able to live up to. Lorena shunned the negativity of logic not to tarnish the joy of possibly her last chance of happiness, which hit her like a freight train.

Lorena found herself drifting away to the deserted ocean beach, not a soul in sight, only her and Douglas. She rested her head on his shoulder, and he kissed her hair. The silence was deafening, the ocean either having fallen asleep or pretending to do so, eager to see what those two would do together when nothing disturbed them.

Douglas put his arm around Lorena's shoulder and gently lifted her chin with his other hand, and she drowned in the radiance of his gaze. Lorena's own eyes sparkled with emotion. She placed her hand on Douglas's cheek, and the blaze consuming his body kindled the flames in her romantic heart. This time Lorena didn't wait for him to kiss her. She leaned forward and brought her eager lips to his. Douglas took Lorena's head into both hands, and their lips and souls connected in a long, affectionate dance. Then he proceeded to kiss Lorena's face, not missing an inch of it. Lorena lay on the sand while Douglas covered her entire body with kisses. It seemed to her that it had been that way all along, and nothing would stop them from staying together till the end of time.

"My darling, darling Brit, my Douglas," Lorena whispered feverishly. Douglas continued to kiss her body until he realized it was no holds barred any longer because she belonged to him.

Lorena opened her eyes, finding herself staring into the front yard through the glass door. Spring had slowly advanced, and the trees had sprouted tender green leaves, rocked gently by the breeze, which was careful not to spook the younglings. To them the breeze was a novelty. It waited patiently for the leaves to grow lest they be torn off prematurely. Lorena looked at the sky, its somber, gray vastness reminding her of the ocean, which carried her back to her daydream.

"Douglas," Lorena whispered, and he kissed her gently on the lips. "I am tired of loneliness, I want to be with you forever. I want us to be on the beach together, holding each other close, with the waves as eternal witnesses of our love."

"Darling, there will never be a day that they won't. You are a gift from heaven, a dream of any man looking for true love. I have walked a long way on the road of my life, which has finally brought me to the light that lit the most distant nooks of my heart where no light has ever shone," Douglas said, putting his arms around Lorena's shoulders.

"I have been craving love all my life, but my heart has never felt its joy," Lorena said. "Now that you have come into my life, your feelings have awakened my heart. It can no longer beat without your affection, without the fire burning in your soul."

"I am here with you, my sweetness, I have entered your life for good, so why do I detect a tad of sadness in your words? Do you have any doubts about my feelings?" Douglas murmured, placing his head on Lorena's chest. She held him tightly, with all ardor of her being that had never known the joy of mutual affection as if afraid to spook her happiness, tears swelling in her eyes.

"Lorena, dear, could you make some tea, please?" The old woman's voice from a world away brought Lorena back to reality.

"All right. Would you like apple or cherry pie with your tea?" Lorena uttered dreamily.

"Apple. I like it better."

"Then apple it is," Lorena said and headed for the kitchen, her feet finally solidly on the ground. She poured a cup of tea and put a piece of pie on a plate. "Your tea is ready, ma'am," she called from the kitchen.

The old woman rose slowly from her recliner, grabbed her walker, and shuffled into the kitchen. Lorena made sure the woman settled upon a dinette chair and then returned to the living room. She closed her eyes again and instantly found herself in the company of her marine engineer.

Douglas sat next to Lorena and took her by the hand. She peered into his eyes, and her face lit up as if ignited by the shimmering smile on his face. He kissed Lorena on her lips again. She smiled blissfully and ran her fingers across his cheek. That fleeting, gentle touch was supercharged with the passion sizzling in Lorena's heart.

"I still love you more," Douglas said teasingly, feeling the warmth of Lorena's hand on his face.

"Then you have no idea how much I love you." Lorena stroked his face again.

She kept daydreaming about her marine engineer while the old woman was having her tea. Once the old woman returned to the living room and settled back into her recliner, Lorena went back to the kitchen and washed the dishes. Her "life in a cage," her voluntary seclusion in the house, turned out to be surprisingly cheerful thanks to the British marine engineer, who was similarly confined to a piece of metal in the middle of the ocean. Lorena couldn't wait for her friend to come back and let her out of her confinement, so she could get together with Douglas or, at least, as close to him as possible. Then, eventually, they would live happily ever after.

Lorena loved Douglas sincerely and utterly, astonished she was capable of such feelings after the pain and bitter disappointment of her relationship twelve plus years ago. Each morning brought a new letter filled with so much love that it was impossible to believe anyone knew so many beautiful, soulful words, the likes of which Lorena had never heard before. With each new letter, her love grew stronger and stronger. Lorena realized there was no return to her previous life, Douglas became her lifeline, and she needed him as much as she needed air to breathe. Lorena couldn't get over the way Douglas introduced her to his little son. "I found me a lovely wife and a delightful mother for you," he had told the boy, who now sent Lorena his greetings every time Douglas called him from his ocean platform. It was so heartwarming to hear that it almost brought her to tears.

One morning Lorena was sitting on the deck, waiting for Douglas's daily correspondence, which didn't take long to arrive. Just like the previous ones, it clouded her eyes with tears.

> Good morning, my love, Lorena! The source of my happiness, the soother of my soul. The peace you've brought to my heart and soul, I haven't known for many years. Since I met you, darling, I have forgotten sorrow existed. I will love you till my last breath. I don't know if I could continue living without your love. Life would be so drab and dismal without you, but deep in my heart, I always believed you existed, the woman God had destined for me, I just couldn't find you. I will never love anyone but you, Lorena. My heart is beating for you and you alone. You are the most precious gift that life could give a man. I miss you badly, my darling, and I think of you day and night. You are constantly on my mind. I love you more and more with each passing day, and that makes every day special.

Words can't express the gratitude I feel from the bottom of my heart for your coming into my life. You are my life, my heart, and my soul! My best friend, my only true love. Today I love you more than yesterday, and tomorrow I love you more than today. Loving you makes life worth living. I don't even feel alive until I see your photograph or write you a letter. A day without you is a day without sunshine, a day without breathable air. When I am cold, I need you to warm me with the heat of your heart. When it's raining, I need you to hold me close in your arms. I need you in my life to fill it with happiness, my darling, Lorena. You bring me joy, you give me strength when strength is about to leave my body, and I am eternally grateful to you for this! You are the best thing that has ever happened to me. Every second I feel you beside me feels like magic, bringing unimaginable glee. Sometimes when I'm alone, I catch myself smiling for no reason, thinking of you. I never imagined ever finding the feelings we share, and I am confident that you are the one and only woman I want to spend the rest of my life with. You've filled my life with such bliss that I don't know any other way of expressing my gratitude except loving you as profoundly as you love me. The world is better with you in it. You opened the door to my heart, dragging the best of feelings out for me to see and be in awe of. I am grateful that you have given me more happiness than I could ever dream of. I want you to be aware of my indebtedness to you for entering my life. My affection for you will never wane, for I am insanely in love with you, my darling. I am lost for words to explain how deeply your words have pervaded my heart. My dear Lorena, you are a love message in a bottle, a dream of love once washed away by the ocean that finally returned to me after many years of waiting. I am overjoyed to have met you at the right time and will praise the Lord for sending you my way. I can't have enough of your being in my life, wishing to be with you on the beach, and I feel heartbroken because you are not here with me. Remember always: this is the man, Douglas, who loves you unconditionally. If only you knew what your love did to this lonely man! You are the only woman for me, always in my heart. Don't doubt it for a second. My love is bigger than any words anyone has ever used to describe one's feelings. Some may say I love you excessively, but that is false because all I am craving is more and more of your love. It may sound trivial, but the phrase "they are meant for each other" describes our relationship accurately. Every morning when I look at your photograph, your stunning beauty drives me crazy, and believe me, that is the best part of the morning. Just like you, I am tired of being lonely. I want to be endlessly blissful by your side. Thinking of you every second. Love you, miss you. Douglas.

Lorena was so overwhelmed that she was unable to move. She leaned her head against the window, looked at the sky, and closed her eyes, drifting away to the distant beach. She visualized a large ship anchored not far from shore, loaded with huge containers. A man was standing on the deck, leaning against the railing and looking at the shore. Lorena peered at the man, trying to take a better look, and instantly recognized her beloved Brit by his gray hair. She waved at Douglas and got his attention. He lowered a yellow raft into the water and paddled toward the shore. Lorena waded into the surf to meet him and hurled herself into Douglas's arms as soon as he stepped out of the raft.

"Here I am again," Lorena murmured, holding Douglas. "I couldn't wait till tomorrow. The time drags purposely long when I'm away from you just to intensify my anguish."

"I knew you'd come. I'm always waiting for you, my love," Douglas said softly, squeezing Lorena. A tear rolled down her cheek. "Why are you crying?" he asked. "We're together, aren't we?" Douglas smiled, wiped the tear with his hand, and kissed Lorena on the lips. She held him tighter, then reached up and touched his face.

"I know your face so well, dear, every little wrinkle of it. I keep staring at your photo all day long," Lorena whispered.

Douglas gave Lorena his trademark amiable smile, took her by the hand, and together they walked along the beach. After a leisurely walk, they returned to the raft and went swimming for almost an hour. Then, exhausted but happy, they collapsed on the soft, warm sand. Curious seagulls gathered around the two lovers, watching their blissful faces, hushed and awed by the affection they never knew existed. Lorena put her head on Douglas's chest and snuggled closer.

"If only you knew how many years I have been waiting for you." Lorena said, rubbing her cheek against Douglas's chest. "I lost all hope, accepted the fact that you'd never show, be with those who never cared for you like I do. All those years I grieved in solitude, my heart weeping tearlessly, while you were somewhere out there unaware of my existence." Lorena sniffled, tears swelling in her eyes. Douglas stirred, raised his head, and looked at Lorena in confusion.

"What's the matter, darling?" he inquired, "now that I'm here with you?"

"But . . . but my life . . . passed . . . without you!" Lorena sobbed.

Douglas looked perplexed, not knowing what to say or do to console Lorena. The seagulls backed off, equally mystified. Perhaps they thought there was only happiness in love. Waves lapped the beach, leaving hissing sheets of foam, as if telling the dumb birds there was no love without misery and tears.

Douglas got to his feet, helped Lorena up, and then guided her into the surf in the hope that the ocean would help wash the pain from Lorena's soul. Indeed, the water worked its magic on her. The waves caressed her body, tossed it around gently, at times carrying her away from Douglas to remind both of them that they could only be happy together till the waves of life carried them apart . . .

Lorena opened her eyes. A bleak dawn was beginning to break, waking the birds. She closed her eyes again, visualizing a small cottage on the beach. She didn't want a large house; all she needed was the love of one marine engineer.

On a large deck, she sat next to Douglas in a wicker chair, holding his hand. The night sky was growing lighter on the horizon in the east. Early birds began to wake up, telling one other about their dreams. A sea breeze rocked the branches, making the leaves aware of the fact that it was what determined their lifespan. The leaves that had sprouted only recently knew next to nothing of the realities of life.

The Atlantic woke up at the break of dawn, its waves roaring menacingly, rolling over one another and crashing on the beach, displaying the unabated strength of nature. The seagulls panicked and swooped toward the house and the two lovers on the deck. The peace that settled in their souls brought them confidence in the life ahead of them. Lorena rested her head on Douglas's shoulder, and he held her in his arms, his embrace tighter and more intimate than anything Lorena had ever experienced. Douglas loved her with all the passion of a man's soul, but Lorena loved him more because it was her first reciprocal relationship.

"Lorena, I never told you this, but I have this fear deep inside that I can't get rid of," Douglas said, breaking the silence.

"Fear of what, darling?" Lorena asked, giving him a quizzical look.

"Fear of losing you, sweetheart," Douglas said, his eyes glued to the horizon. "I'm afraid you may meet someone else and forget about me."

Lorena looked into his eyes and touched his face. "Haven't I told you how many times a day I look at your photograph, etching your image in my heart and soul for eternity? Your face is what keeps my heart beating." She spoke with such feeling that it brought tears into the eyes of her darling Brit.

"Promise you'll love me for the rest of your life, never forget me, and never replace me with anyone else," Douglas said emphatically.

"You and you alone will be in my heart till my last breath," Lorena replied. "Don't ever doubt my feelings for you."

"And I will always love you," Douglas said, putting his arms around Lorena.

"I've never been happier in my life," Lorena said, looking Douglas in the eyes. She wanted to add that the ones she had loved before never returned the feeling, that she had suffered immensely because her love had been rejected, but she changed her mind. "You will never regret falling in love with me. I will dedicate my life to make your life delightful."

"I know that," Douglas said, holding Lorena tightly in his arms.

"You are so handsome," Lorena muttered through her tears.

"That's because you love me," Douglas said, chuckling.

The day finally chased the night away, and the sun peeked out from behind the clouds, lighting up the world. Douglas took Lorena's hand, and together they strolled along the beach, enjoying the cool, soft sand under their feet. Seagulls stalked them, chatting with one another, gossiping about the strange humans' passion, the likes of which they never knew existed. The ocean was waking up slowly, tossing and turning in its sandy cradle, roaring and raising foamy waves to prove it hadn't lost its might overnight. The waves chased one another to the beach, crashing loudly on the sand as if teaching the firm ground who was the true master of Earth. The seagulls took off in a panic, but the two lovers, a Brit and a Russian, didn't seem to be spooked by the ocean's show of force and bravely stepped into the waves, which picked them up and carried them to the land of dreams, where there was love without chagrin, where a heart never forgot the sweetness of lips and the warmth of an embrace. An instant later, the wave swept the lovers off their feet and hurled them back onto the beach as if saying, "Beware, loving hearts, the wave of life may change direction." The wave wrapped the lovers in a coat of foam, reminding them of the torrents of tears that love brings along. Alas, the lovers didn't take the hint, laughing, frolicking, and hugging each other, their lips locking in a passionate kiss.

"My darling Douglas, I love you so much!" Lorena whispered, kissing the Brit again and again.

"You are my only love, God himself sent you to me to forever rid me of loneliness. You alone will be in my heart till my last breath," Douglas replied.

Lorena opened her eyes, took a deep breath, and went back into the house to make breakfast for the old lady. Spending most of her days in front of the TV with the old woman, Lorena looked forward to Douglas's next letter, a magic pill for her loneliness blues.

One time Douglas wrote that his son had asked for the photo of his "new mommy" and that the boy liked her a lot and felt a strong affection for her, which drove Lorena to tears. Once Douglas asked Lorena if she liked wine and, if yes, what type she preferred. Lorena responded that she didn't care much for wine, preferring liqueurs, especially Irish Cream. Douglas said he loved Irish Cream and could easily drink three shots, and Lorena told him that she could do much better than three shots. That exchange amused Douglas because he was perplexed that Lorena could drink that much and Lorena because she was so perplexed by that fact. It was obvious the Brit was unfamiliar with the anecdotal theory about alcohol running in Russian people's veins. That night Lorena got another letter from Douglas.

"My darling beautiful wife," the letter started. Lorena shuddered. No words could penetrate her heart deeper than those. Her eyes clouded with tears. Never before had any man who she loved called her that. Lorena broke out crying over her bitter fate of being lonely, rejected by love, and it took her a while before she could continue reading.

> You have brought untold happiness and love to my son and me! You are my love, my loyal adherent, my today's and tomorrow's happiness. The dark, bottomless pit of solitude closed with your arrival. God sent you to me to pull me out of the swamp of perennial misery. If only you knew how much I care about you, you'd love me even more. I told my son that you were created to make me happy. I would be blissful to see your face every day for the rest of my life, my darling, Lorena. You are the sole joy that I deserve, the joy that fill my entire being, changing me completely. I haven't felt such deep affection in a long while. If I know the meaning of love, it is because of you, my darling, Lorena. All I want in life is you. You are in my heart and in my mind today, tomorrow, and forever. I am so looking forward to meeting you, to having you next to me for the remainder of my life. I miss you more and more with each passing day, my love. Believe in my love, darling. Never doubt it, never stop loving me, and I will love you forever. My heart won't take another heartbreak; next time it will break for good. I wake up every morning thinking of the most beautiful woman in the whole world, proud of being the husband of the most loving woman in the world. You are in my heart every minute and every second. You are made for me; I know it. I haven't felt the love my heart is brimming with now for a long, long time. If you only knew how much I want to be with you every minute of my life! My heart fills with happiness when I think about you. Your love gives me strength, and I will always be indebted to you for all that you have given me. I repay this debt by giving you my heart. My darling Lorena, I am always with you in your heart. You are my

happiness, the joy of my days. I wish that every day of your life is filled with joy, happiness, and love. I want you to know that I love you more than you could ever love me. You are the woman I was looking for, the one I desired. I am dreaming of sharing my life with you. If only you knew how much I love you! You are my sun, my beam of light, my wife, the one and only woman for me. You are the woman of my youth, my dream come true, a woman who has made my troubles and my heartaches disappear, the one who has filled my life with love and joy. How lucky I was to meet you! You know how to win my heart, darling; that's why it's yours now. You taught me and showed me what true love is. You are the only true love of my life, the only treasure and dream that I have. All that's good in me is from you. All I can think of is you. I am grateful for your coming into my life. You have won my heart so suddenly! Who knew I would be this lucky to have you in my life? Now that you've become part of my life, I don't ever want to lose you. You have brought me so much joy, happiness, and love. No other woman can come close to that! You took what was best in my heart and exposed it to me. I wish you knew how much I treasure your sense of humor, emanating from your loving heart. Every time I look at your photograph, my heart beats so quickly, as if it's about to jump out of my body. You are the only one with a key to my heart, Lorena. You always say what I need to hear. I will love you forever, my beloved wife! I am forever grateful for all you've done for me. Life is pointless without you. You have made me whole again, and I praise the Lord for bringing you to me! Your heart is so close to mine that I can almost feel it beating. Your prayers give me strength and help me overcome any hardship. You are the love of my entire life, darling. I don't know how I would live without you, without your love. My life would have been miserable had God not helped me to meet you. I have given you my heart and my strength; you are my entire life! I love every inch of your body and will never be able to forget you. Your love is so immense that I feel it over a great distance separating us. My heart is filled with such boundless joy. Your presence is so immeasurably overwhelming! I am unable to do anything without thinking of you, my love, for you are driving me insane. All I desire is to talk to you, to hold you in my arms, and cherish you in my dreams. I have never felt anything like this in my entire life. Why didn't I meet you earlier? I was lonesome for too long. Loneliness shortened my life by half until I met you. God only knows why this happened. Now I feel stronger, my love, for you have filled me with vigor. Now I can't imagine my life without you in it, without your love and care. Love is the greatest joy of our life. You are my love, my life, and nobody can take you away from me and my son. My entire world, my heart belongs to you alone. I will love you and keep you in my heart for the rest of my life, my darling. I am prepared to pay any price to see you happy till my final breath. If only I could hear your voice right now, to see you, my love! God created you for me. You are the one I have been looking for all my life. I have seen the grace and purity of your heart, my darling, Lorena!

I just couldn't wait to talk to you, my beloved, so I left my friends in the other room to write to you. You are the only joy in my life, and I choose to be with you, my darling!

Lorena was overwhelmed by Douglas's letter. She was still astonished by how much tenderness, warmth, and romance his heart held. She still couldn't believe Douglas was so profoundly in love with her only through letters and photographs without actually meeting her.

Women find it hard to believe a man's soul can be as sensitive, tender, and full of love and emotion as that of a woman. Marine engineer Douglas was the best refutation of this female stereotype. The charisma of his soul, brimming with romance and sensitivity, can only be found in Stefan Zweig's timeless "Letter From An Unknown Woman."

Lorena immediately wrote back.

Dearest Douglas,

From first moment, when you started writing to me, my heart was open. I had the feeling that I had known you for long time, like you were my friend. When I saw your picture, I knew this was the face that I wanted to love forever. I still can't believe you love me. I find it hard to believe that I am loved by someone I love because although some men did love me, the ones I loved failed to reciprocate my feelings. Over the last twelve years, I forgot about the existence of this emotion, protecting myself from another disappointment, another heartache. All those years I had not been close to anyone, for I had convinced myself I was destined to remain loveless. I have learned to deal with my solitude; it is not as scary as people think. With no loved one by my side, there is no deception. With no loving embrace, there is no pain of finding out those arms were around someone else. Solitude and lovelessness even suppresses tears, forcing them to hide in the darkest, deepest crevasses of the heart, which aches and weeps tearlessly for the life that passes without the dream of love coming true. The love I've been looking for remained on the pages of love stories, and I felt like asking the authors where they saw the love they had written about so eloquently and extensively. And why was I left out of it? Am I so different from other women? Indeed, solitude is not as horrifying as some people assume, but your heart grieves when silence is your only companion, and all you desire is to look into someone's affection-filled eyes. You crave a tight embrace, the warmth of someone's heart next to yours. Instead, you are surrounded with a great emptiness for want of the one who has a place for you in his heart. Solitude is scary for novices, but when you drink and breathe it year after year, the heart becomes immune to the affliction of happiness. You hide your feelings behind a smile, the proof that you haven't been broken, that you are stronger than you thought you were. People are deceived by the smile, taking it as a sign of contentment. Yet you and you alone know how solitude tears your heart apart, how your soul yearns for a lover. Solitude is child's play compared to the instant when you learn about a loved one's deception. Solitude is a bottomless abyss, coldness without embrace, eternal anguish dwelling in your heart, but no pain of finding a loved one in someone else's arms when the world you believed in for many years comes crumbling down around you. After I went through all of this, and my heart surrendered to solitude, finding in it a certain consolation and peace, you came into my life with the words unknown even to poets and brought my heart out of a long hibernation. At first it was overcome by fear of being rejected once again, by the dread of living through another heartache, but the panic passed, and soon it fell madly in love with you, oblivious to why and how it came about. If you don't reject it, my heart will keep loving you while it continues beating, and you will never regret it.

Lorena sent the message and then settled by the glass door, waiting for a reply. The clouds sailed slowly across the sky, followed by bigger, darker ones that seemed hell-bent on chasing them away, determined to prove they were the real masters of the spring sky. The smaller clouds scrambled to get away, afraid of becoming overwhelmed by the bullying pursuers.

Lorena watched the wind rattle huge trees, foretelling a deluge, and soon rain poured down in sheets, washing the dust off their branches. A melody wafted in suddenly, the weeping of a violin reflecting the agony of the soul from which it emanated. The tree branches, failing to recognize the angst of the soul, swayed to the melody of someone's suffering, celebrating their sprouting new foliage. Birds with colorful plumage would stop being afraid of the branches, tell them about those who, concealed by the dark of night, were waiting for the dawn with them. Lorena thought about her marine engineer on an Atlantic beach. Perhaps, right at that moment, he had descended to the depth of the ocean, as if there wasn't enough water on Earth pouring down from the sky. In her fantasy, Lorena descended to the bottom of the ocean to meet her beloved Brit. She swam like a fish, perhaps even better, in search of him. Douglas didn't recognize her in the dark, so she swam closer, took him by the hand, her other hand reaching out to touch his face. Douglas smiled as if he truly was in love with her . . .

Lorena opened her eyes to see rain still pouring down in sheets. The violin continued its wailing, accompanying the weeping of spring rain. The birds took off into the mist. They had seen enough lonesome weeping in their lifetime.

All day long Lorena waited for a response from Douglas, but it never came. He was probably tired or overloaded with work, Lorena reasoned, trying to keep her composure.

The following day didn't bring any relief. Her inbox remained empty, and now she was alarmed. Looking at Douglas's smiling face, Lorena uttered prayer after prayer. "God almighty, all is in your hands. We are in your power. Please keep him safe!" She kept repeating those words, tears running down her cheeks. She couldn't help but wonder how that man had become so dear to her. After all, she had never met him in person.

Time flew by, but Lorena's inbox remained empty. Grief settled in her soul, not leaving it for a minute. She was fairly certain that Douglas couldn't have forgotten about her, which meant he could be sick or worse.

Lorena lowered her head, closed her eyes, and found herself back on the beach. The ocean raised mighty waves, rushing toward the land as if trying to teach people not to disturb its peace and fool around in its depths, poking at its soul and discovering its tightly guarded secrets. Lorena faced the waves bravely; they won't scare her. She would never stop waiting for the gallant marine engineer even if it took the rest of her life!

Suddenly, an orange rubber dinghy appeared between the waves. In it was her beloved marine engineer. Unable to restrain herself, Lorena ran into the surf, eager to embrace the one who had become the dearest person in the whole world for her.

She smiled dreamily and opened her eyes, but all she saw was gray, dreary sky. She sighed and closed her eyes again, only to find herself in the arms of her marine engineer, who must have just stepped out of his dinghy. Douglas held her close to his heart, and Lorena, her face illuminated by a blissful smile, kept kissing every inch of his face while the waves lashed at their feet, jealous of their love.

A huge wave came out of nowhere, sweeping the lovers off their feet. Spiting the waves, they laughed heartily, lying on the wet sand until their lips met in an affectionate kiss.

Now every time Lorena looked at Douglas's photos, tears swelled in her eyes, and she began to sniffle. She was scared that he had forgotten her after all. Then what would she do? She couldn't live without Douglas any longer. She was different from the former Lorena, who was lonely and loveless but unafraid.

The abrupt stopping of correspondence from the marine engineer hurt Lorena deeply now that she was used to the new reality where she was loved and desired. Lorena would wake up in the middle of the night to check her mail, but her inbox remained empty. Yet she waited stubbornly for a short message or phone call. The British marine engineer vanished from Lorena's life as suddenly as he had appeared.

At first she invented various reasons for Douglas's disappearance; however, in a matter of days, she was no longer able to fool herself. Meanwhile, the orange rubber dinghy kept appearing in Lorena's dreams. She ran toward it into the surf to embrace her beloved Brit, but the dinghy was empty, Douglas nowhere in sight. She could no longer exist without his love, his tender touch, as if she had been loved her entire life, as if she had never felt the pain of solitude. In two months Lorena had gotten used to the kind of love that she had never experienced. She shuddered, realizing how little she knew about Douglas, practically nothing except his name, the name of his son, and the boarding school he was attending. There was nothing she could do but wait for him to reappear on her horizon.

Time went by, and days turned into eternity because there was no news from Douglas. She kept looking at his photographs, scrutinizing his face and his hands with such affection as if she had never seen hands before. She adored every inch of his face, and it seemed to Lorena that Douglas's eyes in the photograph were smiling at her and her alone. In her thoughts Lorena kept drifting away to the beach, savoring many sweet moments in the arms of her beloved. She would wade into the surf, peering into the waves in search of him, and then, disappointed and heartbroken, sit on the sand with her face against her knees, crying bitterly. The waves crashed on the beach at her feet, spraying Lorena with water and foam, either attempting to cheer her, overcome by sympathy, or expressing their anger. Oblivious to the waves' behavior, Lorena remained unperturbed. Waves didn't frighten her. She was prepared to travel to the bottom of the ocean to find her beloved marine engineer.

Meanwhile, on a faraway beach, when the sun had already retired till the next day, a gray-haired man in orange coveralls was lying on the sand, unconscious, next to an overturned orange rubber dinghy. A beach party of three, a male and two females, spotted the man and cautiously approached him.

"Look, he's alive, his eyes are opening!" one of the women cried. The man in orange coveralls slowly opened his eyes, and his face lit up. He was alive, having cheated death this time. The strangers helped Douglas up, but once on his feet, he lost his balance and had to be supported by the man.

"Where do you live? We'll help you get home," the man asked Douglas, who stared at the women, unable to utter a word.

"He must be in shock, let's take him to my house," one of the women, a stocky, blue-eyed blonde in her sixties, said. The man put his arm around Douglas's waist, and the party made its way across the dunes toward a small ranch a short distance from the beach.

"You're lucky the storm blew over," the man said. "The waves last night were scary. You would have had zero chance then." He helped the gray-haired Brit into a chaise lounge on the terrace.

"We have to go, or we'll miss our bus," the blue-eyed blonde's friend said, giving her a hug. "He's rather cute. Don't let him go!" she whispered. Both women giggled.

As soon as her friends left, the blue-eyed blonde approached Douglas. "I'll make you hot tea," she said. "It will fortify you a bit." Then she went into the house. The marine engineer smiled without comment.

A few minutes later, the woman returned with a large steaming mug. She moved a small table next to Douglas's chair and then set the mug within his reach.

"Thank you," he said and then sat up and reached for the mug.

"Those two are my friends, my girlfriend and her husband," the blonde said, sitting in a chair next to Douglas. "They live a few miles down the beach, so we see each other a lot. I'm Annie. And you?"

Douglas put the mug on the table, squeezed his forehead, with both hands, and rubbed it. "I don't . . . can't remember anything but the storm. I've never experienced this in my lifetime. The waves were as high as skyscrapers. They ravaged my dinghy . . ." Douglas muttered, ignoring the question.

"It's OK, you must rest. Relax out here, and I'll make you something to eat." The woman got up.

"Don't bother, thank you, I'm not hungry," Douglas said nervously.

"All right, then I'll prepare a bed for you. You'll rest and will be as good as new in the morning. It will all come back to you. I live here by myself, so no one will disturb you." The blonde disappeared inside the house.

The next day, Douglas got up early, feeling rested and refreshed. He tiptoed onto the deck, cautious not to wake his hostess. However, Annie was already up, relaxing in a chaise lounge with a cup of coffee.

"Good morning, Annie," he said, smiling. "You're up early. I was afraid I'd wake you up."

"I'm usually up early, before the birds wake up." She smiled back at Douglas. "You know, when birds wake up they tell one another about their dreams, and people think they just chirp."

He laughed. "Then you must understand their language.'"

"What's your name? Where are you from?" the woman asked, noting his good-natured smile and handsome face. The smile vanished from the Brit's face, replaced by a shadow of sadness. He didn't respond.

Annie smiled. "Don't be upset if you can't remember your name. In time it will come back to you; it happens. In the meantime, we'll think of a temporary name, if that's OK with you."

"All right," the marine engineer muttered dismally.

"How about Charles?"

"That's a good one."

"It's settled then. I'll call you Charles."

"Awesome," the marine engineer said, and they both laughed.

Somewhere a long way from the Atlantic coast, Lorena kept her perpetual vigil, from the moment she opened her eyes till late night when exhaustion finally overcame her. But even in her sleep, Lorena found no peace. The Brit appeared in her dreams like clockwork with his charming smile. Lorena rushed toward him with her arms open, hungry for his embrace, but every time she got close, he vanished like a ghost.

She refused to believe that Douglas could forget her. She was too much in love to put up with such a dreadful prospect, so she kept waiting, day after day, week after week. She would sit by the glass door, looking out into the yard at the tall trees, a mute question in her eyes: what had happened to her beloved Brit? Some ghostly force inside Lorena was compelling her to travel to an obscure Atlantic beach, as if Douglas were waiting for her there. And indeed, she would travel there often in her daydreams, to the cottage with the ocean view where she sat on the porch where her darling Brit used to hug and kiss her. Now the cottage was empty, and gone were the chairs they used to sit on while Douglas was pledging his eternal love to Lorena. She walked the never-ending beach, exhausted, searching for her beloved, but he was nowhere in sight. The large ship had also disappeared, but Lorena could no longer imagine her life without Douglas's love, without his beautiful letters. The ocean raised angry waves, trying to chase Lorena away, but the pain in her eyes shamed them into submission, and they kneeled beside Lorena's feet, awed by the love that even death couldn't scare.

Lorena kept living in her past, waking up in the middle of the night to check her empty inbox. All day long she looked at Douglas's photographs, holding his face in front of her every night before falling asleep, weary and heartbroken. And, of course, weeping over his passionate letters.

> My love, my darling, Lorena, all I could think of at work today was you. Come to me, dear. Stay here with me! You are all I have in my life. I love you with all my heart; you know that. I missed you all day long, and although you are always in my heart and mind, I can't wait to finally see you. You are welcome to visit me in my dreams as well. My door is always open for you. I miss you, darling Lorena, the dream of every man on Earth. I am boundlessly happy that you love me so much. I know how strong your love is. I could never love anyone but you now that my lifetime search is finally over! Sometimes when I can't write to you during the day, I feel like I'm gasping for air. You must not worry so much about me; it upsets me, darling. I am still shocked by the stroke of serendipity that brought us together, by the way we connect to each other like

twins. We are truly made for each other. This morning I woke up longing for your kiss, my darling. You will not believe, but that desire was so overpowering that I felt like crying! It will be so awesome when we are finally together, but the moment when I kiss your lips, touch your body for the first time will, indeed, be special. That moment will be so sweet and magical that I can almost feel it here, far away from you. My darling Lorena, you, probably visualize it too, the first moment we meet. That first moment, that first day, promises to be mind-boggling and breathtaking. I can't even imagine the moment of our first intimacy. It will be the pinnacle of our passion as I take you to the stars! When your lips, blazing with love, join mine, which will be burning with the raging desire of my heart, we will create a firestorm of passion, my darling Lorena! You care about me so sincerely that it brings me to the verge of tears, my love. If only you could imagine how much I desire to be beside you, to put my arms around you so tightly that our hearts beat together.

Don't be so worried about me, dear. My work is not as dangerous as it may seem. Besides, I have a guardian angel who protects me from danger. You are that angel, Lorena, the woman I've been looking for, for my entire life. No woman ever cared about me as you do. You've brought so much joy into my life, the joy I was deprived of for many years. You have flooded my world with the light I was craving in my dismal, lonesome existence. God himself sent you to me and made me the luckiest man on Earth! I am blissful to know you are now mine. You wouldn't believe how happy I am to have you. When you meet a woman who loves you unconditionally, you must be blind not to see that.

Lorena, my love, it's dead of night here, but I don't feel like sleeping. I have been so far from you since this morning. If only your kisses and the warmth of your embrace had reached me, I would be sleeping like a log. Your words have reached the very bottom of my heart. Soon we will be together, and you will be in my arms, my darling Lorena. Our hearts have so much in common, they accepted each other unconditionally. My photograph that you liked so much… my dear if you only knew how this man yearns for your love! He wants to be with you till the end of his days! His heart is wide open for you, my love! What would have become of me, how would I have lived had I not met you, darling? Where would I have found the happiness, you have brought into my life? For the bliss you have rewarded me with I promise you will never experience any misery or anguish. I promise to love you till my dying breath. Over a very short time your presence in my life has changed it completely. I wish you knew how happy I am because I have met you, my long-awaited dream has finally come true! To wake up every morning holding you in my arms is the greatest dream of my heart, which is tired of loneliness! My life will be happy because you will be next to me for the rest of my days! I love you for the kindness of your heart, there is nothing more marvelous in this life than your heart. I will love you forever! I can't imagine my life without you! If only you knew how much joy and happiness is my soul, because you love me so much! I will always be with you, I will never relinquish you to loneliness. I will give my life to make your life happy! I am grateful to you, Lorena, for your awesome love, so I promise you will never regret that you love me so deeply. I will love you every minute of every day, I will never tired of loving you, Lorena. I am commending to you my love and my heart, but please be careful to never break it! Remember, my beloved, Lorena that no man could ever love you more than Douglas! I will never forget the day I first saw you, the day I met you! My heart melted when I saw your beautiful face! Through your face I was able to perceive the kindness of your heart. I am happy to have met you, the dream of my entire life, my one and only greatest love. No one, no other woman in this World could replace you in my life. I love you, Lorena and will continue loving you till my last breath. Sweet dreams to you, my darling, remembering that I, Douglas, love you more than life itself.

Lorena closed her eyes, frozen in her chair next to the glass door. Darkness was receding. The birds woke up and perched on wet tree branches, chirping excitedly about heartbroken Lorena.

A sudden gust of wind rattled the branches, shaking off drops of the previous night's rain from the leaves that fluttered, thanking the wind for relieving them from their wet burden. The wind laughed sarcastically at their naivete and then ran away, embarrassed. The fledglings could not fathom the threat of distant fall when they would become wary of the slightest breeze spelling the end of their short lives. Tiny pink flowers on a tall hedge ogled Lorena sadly, regretting their early budding. They must have thought their life was only about happiness, that the sun would always shine for them, keep them warm and cozy. Clueless about the lightning speed of change from bliss to chagrin, they should have queried Lorena, whose short-lived joy had suddenly become perpetual agony.

Somewhere far, far away, in the backyard of a cottage not far from the Atlantic beach, another woman touched the face of the handsome, gray-haired British marine engineer and whispered gently. "Where will you go now? You don't remember anything. Stay here with me. I will take care of you, and you will be happy here." She ran her fingers across his cheek, reached up, and kissed him lightly on the lips. He put his arms around the woman and responded to her kiss.

Lorena wiped her tears, went into the house, and started packing. It had been two months since she had been staying with her friend's mother. Today her friend was coming home.

Lorena returned to her Moscow apartment, burdened with memories. She was completely lost, not knowing what to do with her life. Douglas had vanished without a trace. Lorena ordered his portraits in large format, hung some on the walls, and set others on her desk to see him anywhere she looked. She went to bed holding Douglas's portrait to her chest, and when she woke up, she touched his face, sobbing.

The following month Lorena finally made up her mind to travel to London and visit the boarding school where Douglas's son, Mark, was studying. This was Lorena's last and only chance to learn something about her beloved.

At Heathrow Airport, Lorena hired a cab and gave the driver the address of the boarding school. It was a large two-story red-brick building surrounded by gardens. After a brief conversation with the receptionist, Lorena was ushered into the headmistress's office.

"Unfortunately we have heard nothing from the boy's father in over two months," the headmistress, a pleasant, middle-aged woman, explained. "He used to call the boy every week, but not anymore. Teachers tell me the boy is stressed out, devastated by his father's disappearance."

"May I see him?" Lorena inquired, feeling more bitter than before.

"Of course, madam, do sit down," the headmistress said and then picked up the phone. "They will bring the boy over in a jiffy."

Within minutes, a plump, pleasant woman entered the office in the company of a lanky boy with chestnut hair. The headmistress nodded, and then the woman left the office.

"Come closer, dear," the headmistress said firmly. The child obeyed. "I know your name, but please say it yourself."

"Mark," the boy said, looking the headmistress in the eyes.

"And what is your father's name?" she inquired.

"His name is Douglas, and he works in the ocean," the boy muttered sadly.

"Do you know why I called you here, Mark?" the headmistress asked.

"No. Why, you have news about my father?" The boy's face lit up.

"No, no news of your father, but this woman is here to see you." The headmistress pointed to Lorena. The boy, who must have just noticed another presence in the office, peered somberly at Lorena. She recognized the look. It was endemic in orphans who had never known the warmth of a mother's arms. Lorena had that look at Mark's age. Suddenly, the boy ran toward Lorena, instantly finding himself in her arms. His scrawny arms locked around Lorena's waist in a tight embrace.

"You're my new mother. I recognize you from the photograph my father sent me. I keep looking at it when no one can see. I even prayed that you'd come! But what about my father? Does this mean I don't have a father either? Now I don't have anyone but you!"

Lorena's eyes filled with tears, and she hugged the boy with genuine emotion that the poor child hadn't experienced in a long time.

Lorena had a sudden flashback to her own childhood when, after her mother died, her father remarried and sent Lorena's seven-year-old brother to a boarding school. The poor child, who had gotten used to his aunt's affection (the aunt stayed with the children after their mother died), couldn't tolerate the boarding school's atmosphere and ran away almost every week. Lorena remembered how her father screamed at the boy when he tried to return home. "Why do you keep coming back every week? If I wanted to see you, I wouldn't have sent you off to boarding school. Stay away from here! I never want to see you again!" The incident took place in the hallway, and Lorena witnessed it from the stairwell one floor above. She saw her brother turn around and walk away, his shoulders quivering. Lorena was only nine, but the scene was etched permanently in her memory.

Lorena was so overwhelmed by compassion for Mark that she decided immediately to take him home from the boarding school. She decided that this little boy, the son of her beloved Douglas, would never share the destiny of her brother. She would take care of Mark and warm his tiny orphan heart with the kind of love that she had been deprived of in childhood.

Several days later, after completing all the necessary formalities, Lorena took Mark to Moscow. It helped that the boy was calling Lorena his new mother and was emotionally attached to her.

"Why do you have so many photos of my father?" Mark asked when he entered Lorena's apartment.

"When you love someone, you want to see that person all the time," Lorena explained.

"So... you'll put up my photos on the wall as well?" the boy inquired.

"But of course, dear. You are your father's son, and I love your father very much, which means I love you as much as him," Lorena said.

The boy smiled. "I am glad you took me out of that place."

"Why, was it that bad at school? They didn't feed you well?" Lorena asked.

"No, the food was all right. I can't complain," the boy said. "But no one hugged me there. They treated us well, but we were never hugged."

"Do you like being hugged?" Lorena asked, smiling.

"Yes, very much." Mark smiled back at Lorena. "My father used to hug me a lot, but . . . he works most of the time."

"It's all right, darling." Lorena reached out and brushed a lock of chestnut hair off Mark's forehead. "From now on I will hug and kiss you so much that you will forget the time when you went unhugged for months."

The boy jumped into Lorena's arms, squeezing her with all the strength he could muster. Lorena lifted Mark in the air and smothered the boy with kisses.

"Do you think Father will find me?" Mark asked as soon as Lorena released him from her embrace.

"I guarantee he will," Lorena assured the boy. "Your school has my address and phone number."

Meanwhile, in the vegetable garden next to the cottage overlooking the Atlantic Ocean, the marine engineer was raking the soil with the skill of a professional gardener.

"Charles, you must be tired working since early morning. Take a break," Annie called, spreading a blanket on the grass under a tree and placing two plates with sandwiches on it.

"Yes, love, you're right, I am hungry," he replied. He kissed Annie on the lips and then sat on the grass beside her.

"A decent harvest is what we need this year," Annie said, biting into her sandwich. "My tomatoes are top notch, big and juicy. I sell produce at a farmers' market and usually make enough to last me till next season. It's not much, but it's enough to support me. God himself sent you to me, because I don't have the strength anymore. I'm not getting any younger, you know."

"Don't you worry, darling," the marine engineer said, planting another kiss on Annie's lips and then getting up from the grass. "I'm here for you. Together we'll manage. I want to finish the patch before the heat."

"Did you like the circus, Mark?" Lorena asked, holding him by the hand.

"I loved it," he exclaimed, trying to match his pace to hers. "Especially the horses. I never knew that horses could dance!"

"They trained them well," Lorena said, "If one can learn, one can become anything he wants. When the summer is over, you'll start school. You'll read lots of books and become very smart."

"Will I have to sleep at school again?" Mark inquired in a thin voice.

"No, my dear, you will never have to sleep at school again, ever. You will sleep at home until you grow up and go to university," Lorena assured him.

"I will be a marine engineer, like my father," Mark said proudly.

"Not necessarily, dear," Lorena said sadly, "oceans are tough to reckon with."

The summer ended, and Lorena took Mark to school. By that time he already knew the Russian alphabet and could read at his age level. Little by little he was getting used to the Russian language. Lorena got a job at the local library where Mark would go after school to do his homework, so when Lorena finished work, they walked home together.

Ten years passed. Mark became a handsome youth, almost a carbon copy of his father, and enrolled in university.

Then one morning Mark found Lorena dead. She had died in her sleep, keeping her promise to love Douglas till her last breath.

Meanwhile, thousands of miles away in a small township next to the Atlantic Ocean, at a farmers' market, Charles and Annie were peddling their produce. Annie, excited and happy, counted the money before depositing it in a pocket in her wide skirt.

Suddenly, a party of several men wearing orange coveralls approached their stand, picked up some greens and tomatoes, and handed them to Charles, who was manning the scales. One of the men, the oldest of the party, stared at Charles incredulously for some time until their eyes met.

"Douglas? Jeez, you're alive? All those years... Why? Everybody was worried sick about you, and you've been alive all this time?"

The marine engineer paled. "Richard?" Douglas uttered in astonishment. The men threw themselves into each other's arms.

"Who's Douglas? What's this about?" Annie asked.

"Douglas is me! My name is Douglas!" the marine engineer said happily, but then his face darkened. "My son! My little boy! Dear Lord, what happened to Mark?" Douglas cried in despair, covering his face with his shaking hands.

A week later, Douglas rang the bell of Lorena's Moscow apartment. A tall, handsome young man of about eighteen with a full head of unruly chestnut hair, the spitting image of young Douglas, opened the door. Father and son stared at each other silently for a moment, and then, in a state of total recall, locked in a bear hug, crying hysterically.

His arm around Mark's shoulder, Douglas walked slowly through Lorena's apartment, every wall of which was decorated with photographs of him. One of the two large portraits on Lorena's desk featured Douglas holding the very phone that he had used to send his love letters to Lorena. From the other photograph Lorena looked straight into Douglas's eyes. Douglas picked up Lorena's photograph and ran his fingers across his late beloved's cheek.

"Why did she die, when?" Douglas asked coarsely. "She loved me very much, and I loved her a long, long time ago." The British marine engineer wiped his tears with a shaky hand.

THE WITCH

His words kept ringing in her ears. The previous night, he had come to see her friend and asked her to pass on a message. "I met another woman, and we love each other, so leave me alone. I don't care about you. I can't force myself to love you just because you love me. I don't need your love, and I will not be looking for you because I don't have any feelings left for you."

She tried to fall asleep, but she couldn't close her eyes. It hurt too much. She hadn't expected such an abrupt end to their relationship, although she had known for a while that he didn't care about her. He didn't spare her. He knew his words would cause her anguish, but he had uttered them anyway.

Emily's world collapsed. She didn't know how or why to go on, not while the cruel words kept scrolling through her memory. Oh, how she wished for death to visit her that night, to free her from the choking embrace of her agony and take her away to a distant place where pain and tears would no longer torture her!

"Oh, Lord, have I sinned that much against you?" she asked as she crouched on the floor, weeping, her head resting against the wall.

She kept recalling those cuddly little words he used to whisper in her ear, only now those words were making her soul sore. They were words of pity, not love. She knew it now, having finally learned the truth from Maria, the friend who had relayed his message to Emily. He had called her many times to say he didn't love her, but every time he had heard her sad, tragic voice on the phone and felt her stubborn love, he changed his mind and uttered the cuddly little words in lieu of the harsh truth. And poor, trusting Emily took those words and ran with them, savored them, and stashed them lovingly in the jewelry box of her mind. Only later did she discover that all her cherished gold trinkets in that box were worthless brass scrap.

He had offered to remain friends with Maria. If she wouldn't mind, he would still come and visit her sometimes, as before. Except now he would be bringing his new lady friend along, on the condition that Maria never mentioned Emily in front of his new love. He was burying Emily alive, discarding her like an old, useless household item and was asking Maria's permission to do it. Moreover, he had the nerve to hint that he wouldn't mind meeting with Emily on "friends only" terms—that is, if Emily wished. However, she would have to put up with his new lover and be nice to her!

Pain and hurt were strangling Emily. Her heart ached, but even the fanciest medicines couldn't control her pain. She felt completely disoriented, like a little child who had suddenly woken up in the middle of the dark woods on a moonless night. Until yesterday, Emily could at least fool herself. She had held onto the hope that things could be fixed between them and dangled the nebulous promise of happiness in front of herself. Now she was deprived even of that little privilege—to fool herself. He loved the other woman a lot, perhaps even as much as Emily loved him!

It was five in the morning when Emily realized she had lost her battle with insomnia. She decided to take a walk. It was dark, and the streets were deserted. She started down the sidewalk, her head heavy from lack of sleep, her eyes burning with tears, and the dull needle of pain jabbing her heart.

She had no idea how far she walked. A new day was dawning. The sky was taking on lighter shades of blue, and the black city skyline was printed distinctly on the heavenly cobalt canvas. Exhausted, Emily lowered herself on a bench under a sprawling tree and stared vacantly in front of her.

"Are you alright, child?" a woman's voice inquired from somewhere next to Emily. Suddenly, Emily felt a hand touch her hair. She started and turned toward the voice. A stocky, gray-haired old woman was sitting on the bench next to her. "What's wrong, dear?" the woman asked. "You were moaning so loudly that I thought you were in pain.

You really shouldn't be out here alone at this hour. You never know what might happen." She paused and peered at Emily's face.

A fresh rush of emotion overcame Emily, and she burst into loud sobs. The old woman moved closer and hugged the crying girl. "Come, now, child. All will pass; just wait and see. Believe me, I know." The old woman stroked Emily's hair. Emily shook her head and kept on crying. "Come with me, child, you must calm down," the woman said, rising.

"Where?" Emily asked, wiping her tears.

"To my house, right there. I saw you from my window and wondered who was on my bench at this early hour. Come, don't be afraid. I'm all alone in the house."

Emily followed the woman into the tiny, cozy house. The woman showed Emily to the kitchen and seated her at the table. "Have a seat, dear, and calm down. When you're my age, you'll understand that all happiness and pain passes eventually. What's your name?"

"Emily."

"And you can call me 'Granny.' I'm alone. I never had any children, and my husband passed away several years ago. Now I'm waiting to join him. He was a good man and loved me dearly." Granny had a kind, pleasant face, and Emily mellowed as if in the company of a close, compassionate relative.

The old woman placed a small tray of cookies on the table and poured steaming tea into cups. "Here, have some tea, child, you'll feel better." Granny smiled, placing a cup in front of Emily. "Thank you, but I doubt anything will make me feel better now," Emily said, smiling sadly.

"I hate to pry, child, but have you had a death in the family?" Granny asked, looking Emily squarely in the eye.

"Yes and no," Emily said, avoiding Granny's stare.

"I don't understand," Granny said, a puzzled look on her face.

"He doesn't love me, Granny. He doesn't love me, and I have no idea how to carry on." Emily finally looked up at Granny.

"Uh-huh. Love is serious business, child. When you stop loving someone, that's final," she said pensively. "Would you like a reading?"

"A reading?" Emily exclaimed in bewilderment. "I . . . I've never really believed in that nonsense."

"Call it nonsense; call it what you wish," Granny pursed her lips. "We shall take a look right now and find out." She rose from her chair and left the room, returning a minute later with a stack of Tarot cards. Granny laid out the cards and made several manipulations that Emily didn't understand.

"You're right; he doesn't love you. He's seeing two women. One is older than the other, with short, dark hair, slightly on the plump side. The other is young, slender, and blond. He is closer to this one, actually. Besides sex, they also have a business relationship. She has brought him much fortune, but he has already had some problems because of her."

"Hold it, Granny. He said he was in love with one woman only," Emily said.

"Nah, he doesn't love anyone, dear. His is the kind of love that dogs have, a mating instinct. Of course he doesn't love you, silly, and you're dying for him! What did he do to deserve your love?" Granny inquired sternly, glaring at Emily.

"How do you know all this?" Emily asked defensively.

"It's all in the cards. Runs in the family, I guess. My grandmother was a real expert, passed it on to my mother, and now here I am." Granny cracked a sly, tiny smile.

"I wonder if . . . I wonder if I can learn it," Emily said suddenly.

"Why, didn't you just say you don't believe in this nonsense?" Granny asked, winking at Emily.

"Could you teach me, please?" Emily pleaded. "I really want to learn."

"That's not all I can do," Granny said. "I can also, you know . . . change things if I don't like the way they are."

"Change things?" Emily repeated, then jumped to her feet and hugged Granny tightly. "Dear Granny, please, please teach me how! I beg you!"

"Do you wish he were dead?" Granny asked, peering intently at Emily as if trying to read her mind.

"No, no! Of course not!" Emily broke her embrace, horrified at the thought. "I wouldn't be able to live if he died."

"He's already as good as dead for you," Granny said.

"But that's different. No, all I want is for him to be lonely, unloved! I want all the women he desires to turn away from him the way he turned his back on me!"

"That's a lot to ask for," Granny muttered.

"He said he loved me. He was so loving and attentive, and then he dropped me like a hot potato. Yesterday, he told my friend he never loved me, never cared for me. All the words of love he said were out of pity. And now... now he's in love with another woman and has never been happier. How could I know that his soul was the color of his eyes—as black as the pitch-dark night?" Emily's shoulders began to twitch.

"Come, now, child. Don't give him so much credit. He's in love with no one. I already told you what kind of 'love' he worships. He doesn't deserve a single tear, a single sigh! Tell me honestly, do you wish he were dead?" Granny asked again with grave seriousness.

"No, Granny. Death is not as terrifying as it's portrayed. Life offers many more frightful things than death," Emily said soberly.

"Well, I have no heirs to pass my knowledge to. It would be a waste if I took it all to the grave with me, wouldn't it? All right, but you'll have to write word for word all that I'm about to say."

Granny disappeared into the living room and soon returned with a notebook and a pen. "Remember! Word for word!" she said sternly, placing the notebook and pen in front of Emily. Intrigued and terrified, Emily diligently wrote down everything the old woman said.

"That's all I know," the old woman concluded, wiping perspiration from her forehead. She looked exhausted and pale. "Now you have the knowledge, and you possess the secret. For your own sake, keep it to yourself. Great disaster will befall you if you don't."

"I will kill him, Granny, but not physically, no! He will wish for death to visit when I'm through with him!" Emily's cheeks were flushed, and her eyes lit up with evil sparkles. "I don't remember my grandmother, but I will love you like my very own till the end of my life if the curses work."

"God bless you, child. The curses will work as long as you believe in them."

Having parted with Granny, Emily rushed to Maria's house. She was afraid Maria would leave for work before she could talk to her, but to her relief, she was still home.

"Geez, you're early, girl!" Maria gasped, opening the door. Emily went into the living room and dropped onto the couch, catching her breath.

"I was rushing," Emily said. "I wanted to catch you before work."

"You OK after . . . yesterday?" Maria dropped onto the couch beside her friend.

"Couldn't get a wink all night," Emily said with a sigh as she stared at the carpet. "I have a favor to ask. Remember he said he wanted to . . . you know, stay friends with you?" Maria nodded, her eyes wide in bewilderment. "Anyway, I want you to say yes. Let him come with that—his tramp—to visit you, all right?"

"Are you kidding? I can't stand the bastard! Never liked the type. You know that." Maria shook her head indignantly.

"Please? For me?" Emily looked at Maria with puppy-dog eyes.

"I don't get you, girl," Maria said reproachfully. "This is absurd."

"Well, just call him, OK? Invite him over sometime this week. I just want to see what she's like."

"I still don't get it, girlfriend. Just forget the jerk. Get him out of your system. He's not worthy of you. He's an empty shell. Take off his expensive clothes and all the glitter, and the polish is gone," Maria argued.

"I'll forget him all right but later. Meanwhile, please do me this one favor, OK?" Emily stood up. "Well, I'd better be going now. You'll be late for work."

When Emily opened the door of her apartment, she was attacked by images of him. He was smiling at her from photographs, hugging her, kissing her, and pretending to care. Emily tore the pictures off the walls, the dresser, and the nightstand, and threw them to the floor. She found his shirts in the closet and ripped them off the hangers with disgust.

"Jerk! Bastard! You never loved me!" Emily cried, assaulting the expensive fabric with her fingernails.

When the outburst of anger subsided, Emily picked up one of the shirts from the floor and fell onto the couch, burying her face in the fine cotton that still bore the faint scent of his cologne. She lay face down, motionless, for a long time, her eyes closed.

How long ago was that night? Emily had been at the breakfast table in his kitchen, a glass of pinot grigio in her fingers. He came over to her side, knelt beside her, and took her free hand in his. "Kiss me, Emily," he said softly. She smiled and bent forward obediently, reaching for his lips. Their lips touched. A light, tender kiss was a spark that set them both on fire.

He brought his lips to her ear, whispering passionately. "Don't go. Please stay with me tonight. I want you badly, darling, I'm losing my mind!"

Somehow, before that night, Emily hadn't realized how much desire could be put into so many simple words. Emily blushed and looked at him coyly. His eyes were pleading. How could she say no? Throughout their relationship, she had never loved or desired him as badly as she did that night. And then . . . the phone rang, shattering the palpable tension in the dimly lit kitchen. He picked up the cordless from its wall cradle.

"Hello. Who? Yes, she's here. It's for you, darling." He handed the phone to Emily and then retreated into the living room to giver he some privacy.

"Hey, I've been waiting for you all night, dammit! Don't you think you're a bit late?" Maria's angry voice rang in the receiver.

"I think I'll stay here tonight," Emily said apologetically. Sometimes her domineering friend's straightforwardness frightened her.

"Let me get this straight. You're staying with a guy you barely know, the one you met just last week? That's insane, girl!"

"You know, I have the weirdest feeling I have loved him all my life," Emily replied, "like I've been waiting for him all along."

"I got it. Prince Charming. Fine. But don't come crying on my shoulder when he dumps you!" Maria yelled and then hung up.

What ominous, outrageous words! Emily's common sense was shut down.

He stood by the door as if blocking Emily's possible retreat, resplendent in a stylish, expensive jogging outfit that emphasized his staggering attractiveness. A hunk. Retreat was nowhere in Emily's mind. She was devouring him with her eyes, loving every spot, every muscle of his body. She had no idea she was capable of desiring someone so much, especially if that someone had just popped into her life.

That night was special, out of this world, unlike any nights that followed. It seemed like a powerful, invisible force was pulling them together. He had asked Emily to stay, and that was all she wanted in the entire universe. Had he been faking then, or was he simply burning up with primitive animal lust? "Puppy love," Granny had called it. Or perhaps he was truly in love with her for that one night. Whatever it was, he had forgotten it and erased that night from his memory. But Emily would never forget his burning lips or the passionate loving that made her body feel weightless, the blissful moments of climax that almost made her faint! He covered her body with kisses, repeating her name again and again.

"Marco, my love, how will I live without you and yet carry you in my heart?" Emily sobbed, soaking his shirt with her tears.

She had been so happy with him. She had loved being in love and was confident that the feeling was mutual. Marco was a courteous lover and knew all the right moves and hot buttons. Not exactly spoiled by male attention, Emily savored his civility (a door politely opened for her, a hand properly extended when she stepped out of the car, etc.), which she mistook for signs of true affection. Oversensitive and cautious, Emily never went out with men if she didn't feel genuinely attracted to them and if she didn't feel the reciprocity. Unfortunately, once the reciprocity was manifested and became a pattern, her judgment became fatefully impaired. People who were unable to lie in a relationship had tunnel vision. For some reason that defied common sense, they could never fully comprehend, even if someone made it a lifelong mission to explain it to them. They could not understand why the other party would lie to them and continued to dwell in a realm of blissful ignorance, oblivious to the truckloads of fraud dumped on their doorstep.

Marco was the opposite of Emily. He would normally fancy nine out of every ten women he met, but he never stopped there. He would relentlessly pursue each one until she gave in. Quickly bored, he moved on to the next woman. His handsome, polished, athletic shell contained a soul the size of a peanut, dwarfed by a humongous ego and a petty, vengeful nature. Marco never forgot an insult, and he punished offenders mercilessly, taking genuine pleasure in his revenge.

As much as Maria hated the idea, she finally decided to invite Marco and his new girlfriend over. The woman was a typical young, blond, blue-eyed, skinny bimbo with no comprehension of anything existing beyond her realm of partying, fashion magazines, beauty salons, and fancy diets. Oblivious to Maria's presence, the lovers were all over each other throughout the evening, kissing, hugging, and whispering in each other's ears. Watching the couple, Maria had no doubt that had she left them alone for a couple of minutes, they would have jumped on the opportunity to make love right there on her couch with all the lights on.

Marco was his usual jerky self. Self-assured and courteous, he seemed obsessed with the blonde as if Emily had never existed. Emily showed up almost immediately after Marco and his girl left, as if she had been hiding in the bushes next to Maria's driveway waiting for them to leave.

"You think he's in love with her?" Emily asked, hoping for a negative answer.

"I have no clue," Maria said. "But love or no love, they seemed very much involved with each other. In fact, I was expecting them to make love on the couch right in front of me." Maria's voice was filled with contempt.

Emily paled, and her lips began to quiver. "I have no idea how I'm going to deal with it," she whispered.

"I told you, give it up. Let him go already. He's not coming back to you no matter what you do." Maria put a sympathetic hand on Emily's shoulder.

"I wish I could," Emily said with a sigh. "But my life won't be the same without him. He just won't leave my heart."

"Well, bury your heart then, and he'll be gone."

"I'll bury it," Emily said thoughtfully. "I'll try really hard."

Emily spent the rest of the night poring over the notes she had taken at Granny's house. She was facing three days of fasting, the first step into the mysterious realm of witchcraft. Hunger wasn't a problem. Every time Emily went through an emotional meltdown, she'd lose her appetite completely. She would brave the hunger. Hunger was nothing next to the anguish she was experiencing.

Marco, her Marco, had dumped her for another woman. Outrageous! He actually had the nerve to kiss and hug that bimbo right in front of Maria! Well, Emily's time would come. She would make him answer for every kiss and every hug on Maria's couch. He'd regret it bitterly, but it would be too late. She'd show him she was capable not only of love . . .

That night, Emily couldn't fall asleep. She took some pills, but the sharp needle in her heart wouldn't stop jabbing.

At the crack of dawn, Emily got up and went to work, as usual. She put on a white coat, tucked her hair under a white kerchief, and plunged into her favorite routine. Emily baked cakes. Not the ordinary, boring ones found on a supermarket shelf but made-to-order cakes for weddings, birthdays, and other rare and festive occasions. She was the "Michelangelo of baking," as her coworkers called her. Dough was her canvas, and frosting, chocolate chips, sprinkles, and syrup were her paints. Emily never just "baked"' she created sweet masterpieces, pouring her soul into each and every one of them like a true artist. Birds really "flew" across the turquoise sky of the glaze, the ocean "breathed," the flowers "bloomed," and the gummy dewdrops looked as if they were about to roll off the tender petals of butter roses.

That day, Emily was withdrawn and somber, avoided conversation, and explained that she was not feeling well. Hunger crept up on her, getting stronger with each passing hour. Sweet, appetizing aromas filled the bake shop, threatening to break her resolve. To stifle the sucking feeling in her stomach, Emily drank water by the gallon. By the end of her shift, she was almost ready to faint.

When she returned to her apartment, she marched straight into the kitchen, opened the refrigerator, and began to unload groceries onto the kitchen counter.

"Hold it, lady," Emily said to herself. "You can handle it. Come on!" She put the groceries back in the refrigerator and poured herself a glass of water. It was only three days of fasting, Emily reasoned. Then, once it was all over, it would be back to normal life again. She could do it.

And she did do it. Once step one was over, she had to do step two, compared to which three days of hunger were a cakewalk. The thought of the next step made Emily shiver, but there was no stopping now. Her biggest fear was that she'd chicken out and break the sequence, leaving Marco unpunished. The thought of him carrying on with his playboy lifestyle while she was agonizing over the breakup drove Emily crazy and fueled her resolve. Somewhere deep inside, Emily doubted the powers of witchcraft, but she used all her willpower to kill those doubts, remembering rule number one laid out by Granny: where there is no faith, there is no power.

The following Monday night, when the clock struck 11:00, Emily left the house. She had a long way to walk, but she had to the cemetery before midnight. Emily knew the town like the back of her hand, having walked every street and alley during her frequent nocturnal escapades.

The closer she got to the old cemetery, the more frightened she became. Her legs felt as heavy as iron, and Emily had to make an almost superhuman effort to move them. She almost chickened out twice, but every time the thought of him entertaining some tramp and having a good time strengthened her determination, pushing Emily closer and closer to her destination.

It was a quarter to midnight when Emily reached the cemetery's wrought-iron gate. The moon was shining its dim yellowish light upon the old church by the gate. As far as the eye could see, endless rows of tombstones stood like silent guardians of the dead. Her body covered by goose bumps, Emily started walking among the tombstones, peering at the dates. Before midnight, she had to find the grave of a man who was Marco's exact age. She was lucky, or perhaps the dark forces were already at work, steering Emily toward the inevitable.

"Charles Hunt," the inscription above the dates on a massive granite obelisk said. The dates were an exact match. Her hands shaking, Emily fumbled in her pockets for the candle and a book of matches. She was afraid that the cool, musty breeze blowing through the cemetery would put out the candle, but to her utter surprise and horror, the breeze died at the first strike of the match. The candle, placed at the bottom of the obelisk, burned evenly, its flame never flickering, as if in a tightly sealed room.

Emily knelt by the candle and began whispering the invocation, word for word, just as Granny taught her: "I, Emily, have come to thee in the dead of night to break not thy repose but to take the oath of a witch. I invoke thee, the forces of darkness, and implore thee to share thy knowledge, to grant me thy gift of witchcraft. I swear before thee who dwell in the darkness of the grave that I shall never reveal my secret. I have come to thee not with fear in my heart, and I shall leave without looking back, endowed with the knowledge and power I sought from thee. I invoke thee, I invoke thee, I invoke thee!"

Emily screamed the last words, waking up the echo that reverberated in the somber field, bouncing between the tombstones. She closed her eyes, expecting some sort of supernatural effect to occur, but nothing happened, only the breeze, which picked up and blew out the candle.

Emily didn't look back all the way home, although the temptation to do so was enormous. Sometimes she heard the shuffling of feet behind her and imagined a crowd of ragged, festering bodies closing in on her, their mummified hands reaching for her. Her heart was beating like a drum, and her skin was crawling with goose bumps, but Emily resisted the temptation, knowing that if she looked back even once, the circle would be broken, and she'd have to start all over.

Once at home, she fell asleep the second her head touched the pillow, something that rarely happened, but her dreams were filled with such horrible nightmares that she woke up screaming.

The next night as the clock struck midnight, Emily ventured out of the house again. This time, she didn't have to walk far. Her destination was a small garden behind the building. She was carrying a paper bag with a kitchen knife and a photograph of Marco inside.

Emily stood behind the tallest tree in the garden, making sure no one could see her from the windows. Then she took out the kitchen knife, cut out a rectangular piece of soil, and placed Marco's photograph into the "grave." When all was done and a large stone was placed on top of it, Emily knelt by the tree and whispered the words of the curse. "I, Emily, am burying not this picture of Marco but his peace. May his every dream be filled with horrible nightmares from now on, as long as his picture is buried . . ."

Once Emily finished the curse, she returned to her apartment. She slept well that night, deeply and dreamlessly.

Over the next little while, Emily changed. She spent hours studying herself in the mirror, but the change was not in her appearance. It was somewhere deep inside, in her character, her attitude. She started to avoid people, shied away from conversation. Maria was her only friend now, and only because Maria didn't try to get inside her like the others, didn't pester her with silly questions.

Every night before going to bed, Emily lit five candles on the floor, placed Marco's photograph in the middle of the circle, and intoned the curses: "May Marco's every hour be filled with as much pain and suffering as he brought into my life! May he be rejected by every woman he wants..." She was committing the man she cherished more than her own life to solitude and anguish.

On a warm summer day, Emily was walking through the park on her way home. Suddenly, she saw a young girl on a bench under a sprawling tree. The girl's shoulders were twitching, and although her head was bent low, Emily could see she was crying. In an instant flashback, Emily remembered herself, tormented and miserable, on a bench just like that, crying her eyes out.

"Are you alright, Miss?" Emily settled on the bench next to the young girl. "Why are you crying?" The girl kept sobbing without paying attention to Emily's question. Then, raising her puffy, wet, yet very pretty face, she looked at Emily with such pain in her eyes that Emily's heart skipped a beat.

"I'm sick. Someone gave me a bad disease."

"You mean . . . how bad is it?" Emily asked, a crazy, ugly, but extremely tempting thought flashing through her mind.

"Really bad. There's no cure." The girl's face became distorted by agony and fear. "I'm doomed!"

"But you're too young and beautiful to die!" Emily exclaimed. "There must be something . . . some kind of cure!"

"They say there are drugs that can prolong my life, but they're very expensive, and I'm broke." The girl shook her head bitterly.

Suddenly, a plan took shape in Emily's head with crystal clarity. "I can help you if you help me," Emily said, moving closer to the girl. "Help me, and I'll give you money to buy the medicine to prolong your life, and then, who knows? Perhaps, one day there will be a cure!"

The girl looked at Emily as if she had just told her she was an alien. "Me? Help you? How?" the girl stared at her in utter bewilderment, but Emily noticed a sparkle of hope in girl's eyes.

"I know how you feel, dear. Trust me, I do. You're hurting inside, just like I am, only for a different reason. Will you help me?" Emily looked at her quizzically.

"But what could I possibly do to help you?"

"Well, for instance, you could meet a certain man, spend a couple of nights with him, and give him what you have. That's all. Do that, and I'll pay for your treatment. What have you got to lose?" Emily said hotly, her face flushed.

"But this ... guy, he'll be doomed too!" the girl exclaimed, horrified.

Emily shrugged. "We're all mortal, so every one of us is doomed eventually. I just want to see him suffer for all the pain I've gone through," Emily said bitterly, looking away.

They fell silent for a while, deep in their own sad thoughts.

"How many times do I need to meet him?" the girl asked suddenly, breaking the silence.

"Not many. He won't waste much time on romance. He'll wine and dine you and take you out to shows and stuff. Chances are, he'll take you to a bar on the first day, then over a couple of drinks he'll tell you how gorgeous, intelligent, and unique you are. Then, if you're mellow enough, he'll take you in his expensive car to his big house, show off his wealth, and tempt you with a promise of it. Then, if he hasn't changed his pattern, he'll beg you to stay the night because he's never ever wanted anyone as badly as you. In the morning, he'll serve you coffee and croissants in bed, then tell you he's very, very busy even if it's the weekend. On this pretext, he'll show you out with a promise to call. If you're really good in bed, he'll probably use you a couple of more times until he finds another toy." Emily paused, then added bitterly, "And this is the man I loved!"

"Do you still love him?" the girl asked. Curiosity returned to her with the promise of hope.

Emily laughed. "Silly, would I go through all this if I didn't?"

"Aren't you afraid of what you're doing? You may feel sorry for it eventually, but it will be too late."

"Perhaps. But I can't stop now; I just can't." Emily swallowed hard. "You'll have to dye your hair blond first. He'll chase after you like a bull charging red cloth. By the way, I'm Emily." She smiled at the girl.

"And I'm Tara," the girl said, wiping her face with a tissue. "You have a deal."

Emily had hardly stepped into the hallway of her apartment when her phone exploded with a high-pitched shriek.

"Guess what?" Maria asked, bursting with news that she couldn't wait to share. "I saw Marco today! I ran into him in the mall parking lot. Here comes the best part: He wasn't alone!"

"Boy, that's a surprise," Emily said sarcastically.

"Just shut up and let me finish. He wasn't with the blonde! The girl he was with was short and chunky with dark curly hair! Boy, was he unhappy to see me! The jerk didn't know what to do. He pretended he wasn't with her, of course, but I saw her stop and wait for him while he slowed down and tried to keep a distance. I have to tell you, he fooled me. I thought he was really into that blonde that he brought to my house. He's going through them like socks! I can't believe you flipped for that worm!"

Emily sighed. "I can't believe it either."

That night before going to bed, Emily lit five candles on the floor and took a shopping bag out of the closet. The bag contained a stuffed doll that Emily had bought at a toy store several days ago—a boy with curly dark hair and dark eyes, just like Marco's. She placed the doll inside the circle of light where she usually had Marco's pictures. In her right hand was a long, sharp needle.

"I, Emily, name this doll Marco. This needle is my heartache. Every time I pierce this Marco with my needle, my pain will enter the heart of the real Marco. I beg of thee, forces of darkness, take away Marco's health! Make him sick, miserable, and lonely! May he always feel the pain he left in my heart!"

With these words Emily pierced the doll's chest with her long, sharp needle. "Marco, you never had a chance to feel your heart before. Now you will feel the pain and find out where it is," Emily whispered, five little candle flames reflecting in her moist eyes.

On Friday night, Emily met Tara in the parking lot next to Marco's favorite bar. The young woman was wearing a tight, sexy, black leather skirt and a thin, white cotton sweater. She was not wearing a bra, and her small, perky breasts bounced under the thin fabric like rubber balls. She had dyed her hair strawberry blond, and her lean face, with a small chin and delicate nose, was skillfully made up.

"Are you sure you want to go through with this?" Tara asked nervously.

"Are you scared?" Emily said. "Even if you refuse now, I'll find someone else."

"What if he doesn't like me?"

"He'll like you; you're his type. He's a predator. He'll look at you like a fox eyeing a plump chicken. Here, take this. Put it in your purse." Emily handed the girl a black object the size of a lipstick tube.

"What is it?" Tara asked suspiciously, taking a step back.

"A microphone. Keep it with you the entire time," Emily said curtly.

"You don't trust me?"

"I just want to hear it. All of it."

Tara shoved the microphone into her purse, and then both women entered the bar through the back door.

The windowless lounge was cast in permanent semi-darkness. Candles flickered pleasantly under orange shades. Mellow, soothing blues poured through the loudspeakers, creating a serene and relaxing ambiance. It was still early for the Friday night crowd, and the women took a corner booth from which Emily could observe the front door without being seen.

Some forty minutes passed before Emily saw him. Her body stiffened, and her face turned pale.

"Is that him?" Tara whispered across the table, her eyes on a tall, handsome, middle-aged man in a blue polo shirt and khaki slacks who had just entered the lounge and headed straight for the bar. His hair was thick, dark, and curly, his body muscular and lean. Emily nodded, biting her lip.

"I can't believe this . . . Lord, help me, give me strength," Emily said in a choked voice.

"Listen, Emily, what you want to do is abominable! I need the money badly, but let's come up with a different plan. Let me tell him how much you love him, how deep your feelings are for him! It may work! You may get him back. You can't just throw it all away. There's always a chance!"

"No." Emily shook her head stubbornly. "I don't exist for him; I know it for a fact. Now, do we still have a deal?"

"Yes," Tara muttered. "We have a deal."

Emily rose and made her way out through the back door. In the parking lot, she opened her purse and made sure that the red light on the tape recorder was on. She listened to it later.

"Do you like it here?" Marco asked.

"Yeah, it's nice and comfy," Tara replied. "I like the ambiance. The music and the lighting are perfect. It's like a fairy tale."

"Every fairy tale has a king and a queen, a prince and a princess. Have you met your prince yet?" Marco asked.

Tara giggled. "No, I haven't been lucky so far. Princes are an extinct species these days. You?"

"Me neither," Marco said with a chuckle. "I'm not too popular with women, I guess."

"Oh, what if you're wrong? What if there's someone out there who's madly in love with you?"

"If that someone looked like you, I'd be in heaven," Marco said with fake sadness.

"How come I would be so different from others?" Tara queried.

"In your eyes I see heaven. I haven't seen that in other women's eyes. That's the difference."

"Perhaps, if you looked deeper, you might see something," Tara said.

"Why would I want to think about other women if the most beautiful girl in the world is sitting next to me? You're not in a rush, are you? It's a long night, and who knows? Perhaps, the fairy tale will have a happy ending after all." Marco's seductive voice trickled through the speaker.

Her hands shaking, Emily grabbed the tape recorder and tossed it across the room. She sat in her dark living room for an hour, maybe more, her hands clenched into fists. It was well past midnight when she rose from the couch, found the needle and the doll, and lit the candles.

A week later, Emily met with Tara and handed her an envelope and a small velvet box. "This is a ring he gave me," Emily said quickly, responding to a silent question in Tara's blue eyes. "Take it. I don't need it anymore. You'll get good money for it."

Emily's heart was acting up more and more. She knew she had some kind of a heart condition even before she met Marco. Now the pain was almost constant. The highly combustible mixture of love and hatred for Marco was fueling her pain. Despite herself, she was still in love with him and was powerless to stop it.

Emily also hated herself for what she had done with Tara's help. She loathed herself for using a sick, desperate girl as a deadly weapon of vengeance. Her only consolation became the nightly rituals, the circle of light, the needle through the doll's heart.

Weeks went by, and one night Emily decided to change her curse. She didn't know what possessed her to do it; the decision came out of the blue. "Marco, I now change the curse and shall not wish thee harm," she intoned, swaying slightly back and forth. "I shall commit thee instead to love me, to long for me, but never to have me. Thou shalt feel the very pain thou gave me, and that pain shalt be the worst, for no pain is worse than the one in the heart of a rejected lover! May this be my last and final punishment for thee!"

Emily pricked her index finger with a needle, smeared a droplet of blood on her forehead, and continued. "I shall rest now under a seal of blood. This seal shall seal the curse upon thee, and may thou always be lusting after me. This shalt be done."

The following night, Emily picked up twelve twigs in the park, brought them home, and arranged them in the fireplace in the shape of a triangle with a cross in the middle. Then she did another chant. "Triangle and cross, cross and triangle, I shall cast my misery upon three corners and four ends. Scatter in all directions, and no matter where he is, find him and make him sad!" Emily set the twigs on fire. "Here comes the smoke, my dear friend. Go fly across the land. Don't go too high, and don't get stalled. Fly and find him in his home. May the sad love dwell forever in his heart, but never tell any living soul in town what we know and what we've done!"

Two months went by. Nothing had changed in Emily's life, at least nothing that could break the routine of going to work and her nightly witchcraft rituals. The pain in Emily's chest was torturing her, but prescription drugs were not helping much. Once during a ritual Emily felt strangely lightheaded. The circle of candles swam in front of her eyes as she chanted. "May he always lust after me," Emily whispered, trying to chase away the untimely dizzy spell. "And may the blood-oozing passion dwell forever in his heart!"

Emily's left shoulder became heavy as if filled with liquid lead. She took a deep breath and got up from her kneeling position. She managed to grab the doorframe when a cold hand grabbed her heart and started squeezing it like an orange . . .

"Hello!"

"Marco, this is Maria."

"I'm all ears, Maria."

"Marco, you never asked me about what happened to Emily after you asked me to give her the message. Aren't you at least curious?"

"To be honest with you, I'm . . . I mean, I was. I was meaning to give her a buzz, you know, but I figured she'd just give me a hard time, you know, start crying and all that, beg me to come back to her."

"She never cried, Marco. She just went all white and couldn't say a word. I thought she'd drop dead right there on the spot, but she lived. She lived to go through that night a thousand times over. She was hurting like crazy, Marco! There was nothing I could do . . ." Maria's voice broke. "She died from her heartache, Marco! Last night. She'll be taken to the church tonight. The burial is tomorrow at noon. Are you happy now?" Maria hung up before he could reply.

Marco's face fell. He hadn't expected that. That was preposterous. Of course he knew that Emily had loved him! Of course he knew she was hurting! An odd, unfamiliar feeling of guilt and sadness crept into Marco's heart. He stood there holding his phone in his hand staring blankly at the wall in front of him.

At dusk, Marco drove to Emily's church, left the car in a parking lot a few blocks away, and walked the rest of the distance. He didn't want anyone to see him, stare at him, and whisper behind his back.

He approached the massive gray stone building from the back and used the service door to enter. In a darkened corridor leading to the altar, Marco found a utility closet and hid inside, placing his ear to the door. He heard heavy footsteps on the tile floor. A priest or deacon was closing up, turning off lights, moving chairs. Finally, the footsteps approached. Marco heard a cough and the shuffling of feet. Then a door slammed, and a key turned in the lock. He waited for a couple of minutes, listening, then emerged from his hideout and headed for the sanctuary.

The church was dark except for the dim light seeping through the tall stained-glass windows and some flickering light in the hall beside the altar. The dark wooden coffin stood on a platform, covered with a white lace cloth. Four thick white candles were burning at the corners, casting flickering orange light upon bunches of fragrant white flowers surrounding the platform.

Marco approached the platform, touched the coffin with his shaking hand, and ran his fingers along the polished side. Emily. His Emily. What did she be like now, lifeless and cold? Did she still have the familiar dismal look on her dead face? Perhaps he should just turn around and run away from this mournful place without looking back.

Marco stood by the coffin, clenching his fists until his knuckles went white. Beads of perspiration appeared on his forehead. Slowly, he reached for the coffin and flipped the lid open.

Emily was resting on the padded silk in a long pink gown studded with knitted flowers. Her face was chalk white, so pale that even the semi-transparent pink lipstick seemed bright on her lips. She looked tranquil, completely relaxed, as if she were sleeping peacefully. She was beautiful even in death, and Marco's heart was suddenly filled with sadness and bitter regret.

"Why, darling, why?" he whispered, touching her cold, stiff cheek. What a travesty. Only recently he had been enjoying the thought of hurting her, hating her for the annoying habit of crying and the sullen, withdrawn look on her face every time he followed a passing skirt with his eyes. The enjoyment was gone now.

"Emily, darling, why did you believe me?" Marco muttered, holding Emily's dead hand. "I thought you stopped taking my words at face value a long time ago! Did you actually believe I fell for that tramp? Hell, no! I made the whole thing up just to hurt you!" He squeezed Emily's hand tighter, feeling the dead iciness of her fingers. "I missed you, Emily. Why don't you tell me it's a lie? It's not. Tonight I will tell the truth and only the truth. This one time only, but you'll never hear it. Here it is: I loved you, Emily. I loved you very much, but eventually, my feelings for you went away, and you just couldn't put up with it.

"Something was pushing me away from you, and your devotion annoyed me! You couldn't explain why you kept loving me. You were always sad by my side while other women were having fun in my company. I realized your sadness was the result of my lack of feelings for you, but I couldn't make myself love you just because you did.

"Eventually I started to enjoy hurting you. Often when I was with other women, I pictured your face distorted by the pain of seeing me enjoy their company. I took pleasure in hurting you. When you fell in love with me, you committed yourself to torment, to death. I bit you like a snake, and you died in agony from the poison. Can you ever forgive me, Emily? With God as my witness, I seek your forgiveness with all my heart!"

When the minister opened the church the next morning, he was shocked and touched to find an athletic, well-dressed middle-aged man kneeling by the coffin, holding the icy hand of the deceased young woman. The priest helped the man up, offered him water, and uttered words of condolence, but Marco did not respond.

Little by little, the church began to fill with Emily's relatives and friends. The service was short, and at noon Emily's body was put to eternal rest at the very cemetery she had visited only a few months earlier, shaking with fear, to take a witch's oath.

Marco stood at a distance from the crowd of mourners, watching the coffin disappear into the bottomless pit and listening to the sound of dirt hitting the top of the wooden box that contained the only person in the world whose heart had been bursting with love and devotion for him.

He recalled Emily's favorite line from a book she always kept by her side. "Gone is my love, gone forever. Bound for the eternity of peace, it hid itself in the depths of the soul, insulted by indifference, so dare not disturb it. Perhaps, it will gather strength and rise again."

A slender, young woman with dark, wavy hair and large turquoise eyes was there every night. Barefoot, in a long pink dress, the woman was invisible to the living and could, therefore, pay frequent visits to Marco's house unnoticed by anyone. She would stand at Marco's bedside, watching him toss and turn. Sometimes he would get up and massage the left side of his chest, moaning from the dull pain, then reach out for the pills and a glass of water on his nightstand.

Then came the night when sirens blared outside the house, and his bedroom was awash with red and blue lights. That night, paramedics entered Marco's house and ran into his bedroom carrying a stretcher and a first-aid kit. They went right through the young woman at the bedside, unaware of her presence.

She watched the paramedics perform their routine, taking his blood pressure, asking questions, and talking on their radios. They didn't take Marco away this time. He refused to go to the hospital, so they gave him a shot, and soon he fell asleep.

The mystery woman in the pink dress sat on the edge of his bed and looked at the sleeping man's handsome face, now distorted slightly by pain. Boxes and containers of multicolored pills were lined up on one nightstand while the other one was adorned by a large photograph of Emily and some roses in a white porcelain vase.

"Marco?" she called softly, touching his hand, which was glued to the left side of his chest. "What's happening to you, Marco?"

"Emily, darling, is that you?" Marco cried as he opened his eyes. "I swear I heard your voice, but I don't see you!"

"I'm right here beside you," Emily said soothingly. "Don't be afraid; you're not hallucinating. It's really me. By the way, did you put the flowers next to my picture just because I'm dead?"

"But you're not dead, Emily, right?" Marco peered into the darkness but couldn't see a thing. "I can hear you, so how can you be dead? As for the flowers, it's... nothing, really. Are they bothering you?" He reached out and pushed the vase off the nightstand.

"You can't touch me, Marco," Emily said, watching him wave his hands in the air in a vain attempt to feel her. "You can't because I'm dead. But you can hear me, and that's wonderful. It's amazing. Regular people can't hear me, even if I yell at the top of my lungs."

"Emily, I'm lonely, and I miss you terribly," Marco said in a thin, teary voice. "I guess I'm dreaming. Thank God for this dream! I'm so tired of nightmares!"

"Marco, I tried to forget you, but I couldn't. You lived inside me, in every cell of my body. I was very hurt when you left me, Marco, and I finally died from the pain. I'm dead now, Marco!"

"Don't talk like that, Emily!" Marco pleaded. "You're alive. You couldn't have died, you hear? I can't take it anymore!"

"You know, darling," Emily said suddenly, "I kept your burgundy pajamas. Burgundy looks so good on you. I wore them every night after you left me. They smelled so sweetly of your body, your cologne..."

"Emily, please stop! I don't want to hear it anymore. You're breaking my heart!" Marco sobbed, covering his face with his hands.

"Heart..." Emily repeated slowly. "Every person has a heart, but sometimes we forget about this simple anatomical fact. Sooner or later we all become aware of it though. When you left me, my heart was hurting. Physically hurting. I tried doctors, medicines, everything, but you were the medicine I needed."

"Will you ever forgive me, Emily?" Marco implored, tears rolling down his cheeks.

"Dead people are forgiving," Emily said sadly. "They have no choice. What's with the medicine over there. Are you sick?"

"Sick...yes." Marco reached for his heart instinctively. "My health, it's all gone. But nightmares are the worst part, Emily. I have them every night, horrible, despicable phantasms. Black snakes with alligator heads chase me, I try to run away, but somehow they're always only a step behind me! It's been going on for several months now, ever since...I don't understand it. I was always such a happy camper, full of life and stamina, but now... First the attacks started, as if someone were sticking a knife into my chest. Then they went away for a while. Now the pain is back. It's always there, ever since...ever since I left you."

"Oh, darling, what have I done?" Emily felt like crying, but she knew she couldn't.

"What do you mean?" Marco stopped sobbing and looked up, staring into emptiness, a puzzled look on his face.

"It's so hard to see you suffer like this, Marco! I've been watching you for many nights now. I see your pain, your agony. I watch you being tortured in your sleep, weeping, crying out for help." Emily's voice broke. "Even in death I have no peace."

"And I have been so lonely," Marco said coarsely. "When you're sick, no one wants to stick around. People walk away from me as if I have some horrible, contagious disease!"

"Those who don't care walk away," Emily said. "That's how you figure out who your true friends are."

"I know. But people don't always choose carefully who to push away and who to keep close. Sometimes it just happens, and then it's too late to fix. But you, you're not going to leave me, are you?"

"Unfortunately, it's time for me to go," Emily said regretfully. "I have to leave before first light. Why do I always have to part with you?"

"Please don't go, Emily!" Marco got out of bed and reached for his invisible guest. "Don't leave me!"

"And why not?" Emily asked, smiling. "You left me, didn't you?"

"Emily, Emily, come back!" Marco dashed toward the fading sound of Emily's voice, but she was no longer in the room. He went to the window and pulled up the blinds. It was still dark, but a thin purple stripe on the horizon heralded the dawning of a new day.

Marco looked at the broken vase and the red roses scattered on the floor, then bent over and picked up a white porcelain fragment. Had he been dreaming? Of course it was a dream, and Emily had never been in his room that night. But her voice was still ringing in his ears; he could have repeated every word of the conversation. The terrifying word "insanity" flashed through his mind.

From that night on, Marco couldn't get the broken vase out of his mind. He was getting weaker and weaker, could no longer work, and his heart condition was progressing rapidly. Doctors were unable to diagnose the cause of his disease, offered no treatment, and advised him to rest as much as possible and keep taking medicine that they knew wouldn't help.

Marco stayed in bed most of the time, getting up only to cook a simple meal or select a book from his library, but he couldn't concentrate on reading. His thoughts inevitably drifted back to that fateful night, a bodiless voice in the darkness, and the fragments of a broken vase on the floor.

Emily walked slowly across the garden in the backyard of an apartment building. It was a full moon, and the garden was basking in eerie, milky light. The trees cast deep shadows on the trimmed grass, but the solitary figure in a pink dress had no shadow. She kneeled on the grass next to a tall tree, plunged her hand effortlessly into the soil, and retrieved a rectangular piece of paper that she deposited in her pocket before floating out of the backyard. She had the ability to transport herself from one place to another through sheer concentration of will. All she had to do was think hard of a place, picture the surroundings, and a force carried her there instantly.

She entered the house through the closed door and approached the bed where Marco was tossing and turning in a cold sweat. He arched his back and moaned loudly, in the midst of a dreadful nightmare.

"Marco, darling, wake up," she said softly. He heard her voice and opened his eyes instantly.

"Emily, sweetheart, is this you?" Marco called, sitting up. "Thank God you're back! I thought I was going insane, but somehow I was expecting you to return."

"I have some good news," Emily said, placing the faded photograph on Marco's pillow. He watched in amazement as the picture seemed to materialize out of thin air. "No more nightmares from now on. You see, those nightmares were part of a curse that I cast upon you. I used this picture in the ritual, but the curse would only hold while the picture was buried. Tonight I unearthed it, so you will be alright now."

"I remember this one," Marco said weakly, carefully touching the picture, afraid it would disappear at his touch or go up in flames. "You took this one at the fair when . . . two weeks before I left you. You were so much in love with me then."

"I have always loved you, Marco," Emily said. "Before and after."

"Even when you were cursing my picture?" Marco asked with a crooked smile.

"Why would I do it if I didn't care for you?"

"I don't know . . . to spite me, I guess." Marco started laughing but then winced and grabbed his heart. "Anyway, I'm not mad at you, Emily. I realized I care too much for you to harbor any bad feelings."

"What about that . . . woman?" Emily asked tensely. "The one you abandoned me for?"

"I never loved anyone but you," Marco said. "I wouldn't lie to you now."

"I still remember the hurt," Emily whispered. "It was I who ruined your relationship."

"Nonsense. I broke up with her myself. Besides, how could you ruin our relationship if I never saw you again after I left you?" Marco said, still not realizing the absurdity of his question.

"The night after I learned the news from Maria, I decided to kill myself," Emily said casually. "But instead I met an old woman, a witch, who taught me the craft."

"The what? Emily, for the love of God, I dumped the stupid bitch myself. We had nothing in common, zero, zilch!"

"Nothing in common?" Emily asked angrily. "If I remember correctly, you asked Maria to tell me that you were in love with her and that you never loved me! Remember the strawberry-blond bimbo from the bar? I hired her to sleep with you, to give you a disgusting, deadly disease! She had a microphone in her purse, and I heard everything. I heard the words you said to her, the sweet fairy tale about the princess and the prince. You repeated, word for word, everything you told me when we first met. Are you going to deny it now?"

Marco lowered his eyes and said nothing. Now he knew for a fact that he was going crazy, but he didn't have the strength to stop the madness.

"So, to cut a long story short, I became a witch," Emily concluded bitterly. "Every night I burned candles and chanted, casting spells on you, sending disease and loneliness to your home. I wished for you to become rejected by women. I wanted them to turn their backs on you like you turned yours on me!"

"Are you happy now?" Marco asked coarsely, without raising his eyes to her. He could not believe what he was hearing.

"Happy? No. How can I be happy? I'm dead, Marco."

"Dead," Marco repeated contemplatively. "Right. So, what you are saying here tonight can't be true. It's absurd, I don't believe in this witchcraft nonsense!"

"Do you believe I'm dead?" Emily asked, amused.

"I guess. I was at the burial, but this is insane!"

"No, Marco, dear. It's the veritable truth. I became a witch but only after you hurt me," Emily said, her voice breaking.

"I'm sorry, Emily." Marco reached instinctively toward Emily's voice, but his hands found only emptiness. "Can we forget about all this? Please? Can we stop thinking about the past?"

"I no longer have any past, Marco. I dwell in a past-less world," Emily said flatly.

"What kind of world is it?" Marco asked.

"The kind where birds don't sing, and leaves don't rustle. It's a world of stillness and solitude. But I have no peace because I miss you, Marco. After all that, I still love you." She started toward the window, went through the glass, and vanished.

"Emily, Emily, where are you?" It took Marco a few minutes to realize she had gone.

He woke up the next morning with a splitting headache. He lay there pondering his strange dream. He had no doubt it was a dream, no matter how real it felt.

Suddenly, a dark rectangular object on his pillow caught his eye. Marco picked up a faded, water-stained photograph. The photograph from his dream! She had made the picture appear out of thin air! He shuddered and dropped the photograph like a poisonous snake. Then he ran to the phone and hurriedly dialed a number.

"Maria? It's me, Marco! I'm sorry, I know it's early, but . . . do you know something about Emily that I don't?" he asked in a quivering voice.

"Like what?" Maria asked, sounding irritated and sleepy. It was five o'clock in the morning.

"Like . . . what was she like after we broke up? What was she up to?"

"She's dead, Marco. What difference does it make? Have you been drinking? Call me at a civilized time if you want to talk," Maria snapped, then hung up.

Emily entered her apartment and sneaked into the bedroom. It looked different now; all the furniture had been changed. She moved closer to the large bed and stood there for a minute or two, looking at a peacefully sleeping couple. Her sister and her family had moved in soon after Emily passed away. Smiling, she drifted into the adjacent den, which was now used as a second bedroom. There, her little arms spread wide and her feet tangled in a Disney sheet, Emily's two-year-old niece was sleeping like a little angel. Next to the little girl was a doll with dark, curly hair. Emily bent over and picked up the dreadful object of her nocturnal rituals, the source of many a curse. An angel girl's bed was hardly an appropriate place for nasty witchcraft paraphernalia. The little girl would miss her doll in the morning, but her childish grief would be short-lived.

Emily went back to Marco's house the following night, holding the doll to her chest. It was pouring, but the raindrops never touched Emily, as if nature itself was showing its respect for a stray soul lost in oblivion. This time Marco was not tortured by nightmares. He was sleeping deeply, but his right hand was still gripping his chest, and a weak moan escaped his lips. Emily recalled clearly the delirium of her rituals, the paroxysm of hate as she drove the needle deep into the soft entrails of the accursed doll again, and again, and again. Now all the curses had come true. Marco was dying, but Emily felt no pleasure. When alive, her emotions were like a seesaw: hate on one end and love on the other, jumping crazily up and down, completely out of control. The new, dead Emily was different. She emerged from the grave a changed spirit, harboring nothing but love.

"Emily, you're back!" Marco cried, opening his eyes. "You're quiet, but somehow I know you're here! I knew I'd see you in my dreams again!"

"Are you still hurting, Marco?" Emily asked, her voice filled with genuine concern.

"Yes, the pain is always there," Marco said, pointing to his chest, "but I think I'm getting used to it."

"Forgive me, Marco; it's all my fault," Emily said sadly. "I have made your life hell."

"Oh no, Emily!" Marco protested. "You can't blame yourself for my sickness. Your witchcraft stories are such silly nonsense!"

Emily released the doll, and it fell into Marco's lap, appearing out of thin air, but this time he wasn't surprised.

"Every night I would stick a needle into this doll's chest, and as I did it, you felt a prick of pain in your heart, didn't you? But then the pain would be gone instantly, right? That's because I'd take the needle out!"

"But now it hurts all the time." Marco shook his head in disbelief. "It's been like that ever since . . . Oh, God, Emily . . . ever since they buried you!"

"I know, dear," Emily said softly. "That's because I had a heart attack and didn't take the pin out. Look closer."

Marco brought the doll to his eyes and saw a red pinhead. He pulled on the head, and the pin came out. "See?" Marco held up the pin. "It's out, but the pain is still here!"

"It's been there too long, Marco," Emily said contritely. "I'm so sorry, but the thought never occurred to me before tonight. I'd have pulled the darn thing out a long time ago! But now I'm afraid it's too late!"

"That means . . . I'm going to die?" Marco asked with childish curiosity as if they were not talking about his own doom.

"I don't know! But now I don't want you to die, I don't!"

"Well . . ." Marco crossed his arms across his chest and smiled knowingly. "That means . . . we'll be together again!"

Marco's funeral was not a popular event. A couple of friends showed up, but even they didn't stay through to the end of the ceremony. None of Marco's former female acquaintances came to see him off on his last journey.

Unseen by the living, Emily stood by the gaping grave, staring dismally at the polished coffin that contained her lover's gaunt, yellowed body.

"Guess who?" a familiar voice said behind her, followed by a hand on her shoulder. "I told you we'd be together, didn't I?"

Emily turned around. Marco, his tanned face beaming with delight, stepped forward and pressed Emily to his chest. She put her arms around his neck and kissed him lightly on his lips.

"Marco, darling, I loved you with all my heart! I knew you were the one for me, my Prince Charming!" Emily smiled through her tears of joy.

"That's why I'm back," he said gleefully, stroking her long, wavy hair.

"In the name of the Father, the Son, and the Holy spirit, take the soul of your humble servant Marco . . ." The words of litany rolled off the priest's tongue, and the light summer breeze picked them up and carried then across the vast expanse of the graveyard

Sleepless Nights

My love,

It has been over a month since you departed from my life. I have suffered terribly all this time, unable to sleep at night, and during the day, I have not known where to run from my pain, which follows me everywhere.

I have tried to forget you, as you asked me to do, but the sleepless nights laughed at my efforts. Like intimate friends, they won't release me from their embrace, not for a fleeting moment. I am so dear to them now. Now I myself am loved—not by you but by my sleepless nights.

Even now as I am writing these lines, they are here beside me. It is night outside. Happy people are sleeping peacefully while others, like me, are writing useless letters.

I am sorry, my love, but I cannot do you this favor. For the first time, I cannot comply, and I refuse to forget you. What could I do when you wouldn't allow me to say your name? I will never utter it again, but I will keep writing letters that you won't receive. They will be read by those who don't sleep at night.

In those letters, you will still be mine and mine alone, loving me as long as I wish, missing me like before, while I pretend not to care, although you know only too well how badly I need you.

Here's my first letter.

Darling,

How are you doing without me? Are you getting along well with the one you love? Do you love her the way that I love you? Do you feel the same sweetness in her lips that I felt in yours when you kissed me? Has your heart ever missed a beat when you put your arms around her?

If you love her truly, then you should be able to understand how happy I was with you. Only, you really don't love anyone, my darling.

You are jealous of my power to love you so much. You have invented something that you have no clue about, uttering different names every time. Forgive me, my love, but I remember every single word you said. Regardless, I do not wish you to be unloved. It is my destiny and my cross to bear. May you never have to feel this pain.

I am writing these lines late at night, when every living creature is resting peacefully. Who are you with now, my love? Do you have any idea how those who don't sleep at night really feel? Of course, you have an unlimited choice of who to love and who to hate, but what am I to do, the one who has none, the one who is missing you so much at night?

Today, I lost it. I took advantage of the fact that no one could see me and cried out at the top of my voice, "Oh, Almighty, please stop him. Don't let him slip away! He has no clue what he's doing! Oh, mighty wind, please carry his brutal words away from me. Howl, bellow, do what you want, but may my ears hear only you! My Lord, please take away my memory, so I may forget the cynicism of his words! For he will be back, since all living matter is drawn to warmth, but I am afraid he won't find me among the living. So, heavens and wind, stop him from leaving, lest you weep over me!"

The wind howled, chasing sand and fallen leaves, carrying them away, oblivious to my plea. The sky frowned, covering itself with clouds, spilling tears of rain upon the land.

My love, I am looking into your darling eyes, and I behold in them a woman not unlike myself, who is missing you sorely and is loving you deeply. Tell me, love, do you recall this woman, or have you erased her from your memory?

I hear roosters shriek, trying in vain to awaken me. Silly birds. They have no idea how badly I wanted them to chase away my sleepless night!

Again, Ms. Insomnia knocked on my door, smiling. "Come in, come in, girlfriend," I said. "You are my closest friend after him. You won't leave me alone, so why don't I let you in voluntarily? Perhaps you'll have mercy on me and leave early."

Insomnia roared with hearty laughter, taking away my last hope of a good night's sleep. "Well now, tell me, dear, why do you fancy me?" I asked.

She shrugged. "People hate me, chase me away. I saw you cry as I was passing by, so I figured, here's a place where I can stay the night."

I embraced her tightly, commiserating with her, for the first time in my life welcoming an unwanted guest. "Insomnia, dear, can you do me a favor? Can you visit my loved one and tell him how miserable I am without him?"

She dashed out through the window but returned almost instantly. "He is sound asleep, wrapped around his girlfriend. Happy people loathe me. Only the lonesome and miserable are my true and eternal friends. So, don't you worry, dear, I will never abandon you!"

"Sleepless nights, cruel nights, get out of my life!" I cried bitterly. "Leave me for good like he left me. I want to sleep for eternity!"

4 LETTERS

My darling,

Are you already up and awake, my love? As for me, I couldn't get a wink last night, thinking about you. I can't wait to see you again. I keep trying to rush the time, but it keeps dragging on, just to spite me.

I'm afraid that the distance that lies between us will ultimately drive you away from me, and I will lose you. Don't leave me, love. I am punished enough by not being able to see you now. Believe me, my darling, no one has ever loaded the word "darling" with as much love as I do now!

Do you remember me as I remember you, my beautiful, beautiful girl? Tell me the truth. At night when you go to bed, do you just pass out instantly, or do you take a moment to think about me?

During the day when the wind touches my face, I think of it as your messenger, sent to bring me your distant hugs and kisses. The feeling of joy overwhelms me. Although it is cold outside, I am not afraid because my soul is warmed by thoughts of you.

I forbid you even to look at other men. I can't bear the thought of your disloyalty. Remember, no other man is capable of the kind of love that I have for you, my darling, my beautiful girl.

And now, close your eyes and imagine me right beside you, kissing your eyes and touching your lips, which burn with love and respond eagerly to my caresses . . .

Love,

A.

. . . .

Darling,

It has been a windy day since early morning. The sky was clear and blue, and the sun was blazing, but its rays bore no warmth. I was sitting by the window watching the trees take a beating from the wind. The squall shook the trees ferociously, as if they were archenemies. It uprooted the weaker ones and tossed them away and bent the stronger, more resistant ones, their roots clinging desperately to the soil.

Some of those trees proved to be stubborn fighters. So, unable to break their will, the savage squall attacked their foliage instead, ripping off their green leaves and scattering them on the ground in frustration.

At that point, it occurred to me that people and leaves are very much alike. The wind of destiny rips them from their branches and scatters them across the world, across the universe. Then a new generation arrives, but the sun keeps on shining, and the wind picks up other leaves . . .

Can we afford to lose each other, to stay apart until the wind of destiny carries us away? I miss you. I miss your lips and your smile so badly that it's killing me.

Love,

A.

. . . .

My love,

Days turn into weeks, weeks into months, and I can't help thinking about you, desiring you. I miss you so much that sometimes I feel like I won't wake up the next morning. My poor heart aches so badly.

I am writing to you every day now, a few lines per day, not knowing if you even care about these letters. Even if they don't touch you, I will keep writing them, for this is the only way I can talk to you.

My love, you are so far away from me, although you live in my thoughts all the time. Why didn't you respond to my previous letter? You know how badly I need your letters! Perhaps, you've met someone else, even fallen in love with him. Don't you dare hurt me like that. I won't survive such a blow! On the other hand, I don't want you to hide the truth from me either.

Love you, miss you.

A.

....

My darling,

Someone told me about you today. Please don't cry for me. It's painful to know that you are suffering so much. Wait for me, love. I'll come and get you. I will take you with me, and we'll be together forever. No force will be able to break us apart. Just wait for me, and know that I love you!

Your letters break my heart. I am touched so deeply by the depth of your feeling. Are you really dreaming of my kisses and my arms around you? My love, all those hugs and kisses belong to nobody but you! My arms will never be wrapped around another woman. My lips will be burning with passion, touching only your lips. Oh, I am so happy knowing that you long for me!

Love me, darling. Love me ever so deeply, just like I love you!
Yours,

A.

....

My love, my darling!

How long since we last met? Days spent away from you have filled my eyes with sorrow. Joy has left my heart, laughing at my grief. With a sly wink, destiny has swapped anguish for happiness.

My darling, I am grateful for the love that you never gave me, for the letters filled with passion and warmth that you never wrote.

All those months without you, I was writing letters to myself, letters "from you," talking about the one and only true love I have dreamed of all my life. Why did I do it? Any woman can answer this question, but here I am, answering it for you. Although, no, this is all so pointless.

I still can't believe you are capable of such betrayal. You, the most heartless, most insensitive of all men! What evil wind carried you into my life?

I was told you said, "Tell her I don't love her." My darling, did I ever have any doubts? I don't understand why anyone would want to scream about it on every corner to make it hurt even worse. You can't hurt me more than you already have. You were broadcasting your happiness to the entire world. You, who live under the sun, should beware of God. God may have far less love for you than I do.

My darling! I failed to stir your numb soul, but there's one favor I ask of you. Please wish for someone to love me as deeply as I loved you, so I can follow him blindly, selflessly. Or wish I were dead. Perhaps God will hear your prayers, and I'll finally be rid of you!

5 The Vincent Island

Vincent Island was astonishingly beautiful. Its majestic, proud, rocky cliffs cascaded down to the foamy turquoise surf. Huge , tumultuous swells of the Great Ocean swelled around it like gigantic muscles. Other islands, large and small, were in close proximity to it. Their inhabitants had either loved Vincent Island or hated it since time immemorial. Like God incarnate, Vincent Island had dominated the surrounding islands, contemplating its neighbors from extraordinary heights.

When something wasn't completely to its liking, Vincent Island simply crushed it with its outrageous might. Therefore, everyone was forced to respect Vincent Island and do as they were told.

At one time, there was another powerful island whose inhabitants detested Vincent Island, but Vincent Island used its substantial brain power (as well as the unscrupulousness of its rival's leaders) to smash the foe into little pieces, becoming the undisputed master of all the neighboring islands.

Vincent Island was stunningly gorgeous. People visiting there from other islands were amazed to see trees with deep purple and crimson foliage, even leaves that were almost black. Of course, there were normal trees on Vincent Island as well, with regular green leaves. In the fall, the green leaves turned yellow, and the entire island looked like the Garden of Eden.

Vincent Island's inhabitants had a special affection for the color yellow. They were so into the yellow leaves that they named streets and even cities after them. Over ten cities on the island were named Yellow Leaves.

Vincent Island was also home to scores of magnificent bird species bursting with festive colors, but the islanders' favorite bird was the one with bright lemon-yellow wings and eyes like black pearls. They claimed it was the prettiest bird on the island, but that was debatable, for who can judge impartially which bird is the most beautiful?

Vincent Island's greatest and most prized asset was, indisputably, its people. Prior to the arrival of the outlanders, they had no idea how fine they were, having nobody to compare themselves to, since few of them had ever left their beautiful island. They were so courteous and good-natured that foreigners found it easy to believe that they were royalty.

Almost every one of the Vincentians had a dark complexion, since the sun had no preference for one group or another. It shone indiscriminately on all islanders, turning their skin either golden or the color of a special fruit that grew only on Vincent Island (the name of which translates as "the color of a ripe peach").

Many residents of other islands dreamed of living on Vincent Island. Under the cover of darkness, they boarded homemade crafts and secretly set sail for Vincent Island. Many of them didn't make it, perishing in the dark abyss of the Great Ocean. Those lucky ones who reached their destination did not realize that the islands they had abandoned with tremendous relief would reappear in their dreams until their last breath. Despite Vincent Island's beauty, the refugees would never be able to forget the smell of their homeland breeze.

All arrivals from other islands were required to have a special "Yellow Leaf Number One." No one could explain the significance of "Number One" because there were more outlanders on Vincent Island than natural-born Vincentians. Nevertheless, the new arrivals stopped at nothing to obtain the coveted Yellow Leaf Number One. For instance, one way they did it was by pretending to marry Vincent Island citizens.

However, the Vincent Island Outlander Control Agency was vigilant. On any given day, any outlander could be summoned to the agency and subjected to a tough interrogation. For example, they could be asked, "What color is your husband's underwear?" It was a trick question, considering the fact that the husband never wore underwear even on the coldest days. But that, of course, was impossible to prove.

On Vincent Island, just like on any other island, people fell in love and got married. However, unlike the other islands, on Vincent Island, women enjoyed unlimited rights. Therefore, when they divorced their spouses, they took possession of everything their husbands had worked for over their entire lives. Many men had nothing to live on after a divorce; they were completely broke. However, the island's laws ignored this fact, maybe because they were written exclusively by women. Because of this, all Vincentian men were scared stiff of getting married. However, as time went by, they tended to relax and forget about the law and fall in love. They were only reminded of it when they found themselves standing in front of the locked doors of their former mansions holding a small overnight bag containing a toothbrush and a pair of threadbare socks.

In one of the Yellow Leaves cities, people were particularly kind and courteous, perhaps because the abundant sun warmed their hearts all year round.

One woman arrived in this city from a remote island where winter reigned nine months a year, and her soul was yearning for warmth. Before Vincent Island, she had visited other islands, but anywhere she went, she felt restless, her soul unable to find peace. Her name was Ofra, and she was a shy, quiet girl. Her soul resembled the petals of a blossoming rose, studded with pearls of morning dew, upon which the shoe of a careless passerby had left an indelible footprint. Ofra bore similar footprints on her soul, but, unlike the fragile flower, she had managed to survive.

Ofra roamed the island, admiring every blossoming shrub, enjoying the spicy fragrance of flowers, and gazing at the awesome birds. She was astonished to see the islanders display their homeland's flags outside every house. *They must really love their island,* Ofra thought. *Because on my home island, people barter flags for bright foreign candy wrappers.*

In amusement and awe, Ofra watched rabbits with pensive black eyes hopping merrily across the manicured lawns and squirrels with long, furry tails parachuting gracefully from branch to branch. *On my home island, people would have trapped these animals, made hats and collars from their fur, and cooked the meat,* Ofra thought.

With deep admiration, Ofra stared at the smiling Vincentian women dressed in long, wide gowns, mostly yellow ones, bearing the picture of a dark-eyed bird with lemon wings—the emblem of Vincent Island—on their backs.

Suddenly, Ofra saw some unusual trees with black leaves, and beside them, other trees with crimson leaves. Some of the trees were in full bloom, swimming in a cloud of pink and white blossoms. One gigantic tree with deep burgundy leaves caught her eye.

Oh, Lord, this is so pretty! Ofra thought as she approached the tree and touched its unusually colored leaves. *I had no idea such beauty existed!*

"Do you like the tree?" someone voice asked from behind her. She turned to see one of the handsomest men on the island. He was tall and muscular, like an ancient Roman, and was wearing an oversized shirt that was the color of the sun and a pair of light-colored shorts. On his feet were burgundy sandals. Most Vincentian men dressed that way due to the heat. The beauty of his dark eyes was rivaled only by the splendor of the yellow bird printed on his shirt.

"You must be an outlander," he said, smiling gently. "None of our local women would be gazing at this tree with such enthusiasm."

"It's just . . . I have never seen trees with red or burgundy leaves. I had no idea they existed," Ofra muttered shyly.

"Yeah, there's lots of things on this island that no other island has. Take the birds, for example. We have birds of every imaginable color."

"It's true. On my home island, we don't have birds like this," Ofra said, staring at the stranger in admiration. He was ravishingly handsome, and his posture radiated strength and confidence. The stranger knew exactly what was going on in her head. He had seen it many times before in other women's eyes.

"Now, what is your name, beautiful outlander?" he asked gently.

"It's . . . Ofra," she replied, her cheeks turning the color of the crimson leaves on the tree that she had just admired.

"Ofra, I would like to make my point very clear. I am Spartacus, one of the richest men on Vincent Island. If you agree to stay with me, I will shower you with money and jewelry." He touched Ofra's hand and looked her straight in the eye.

"I appreciate your generosity, Spartacus, but I have enough of my own money," Ofra replied with a touch of embarrassment.

"Well then," he said with a shrewd twinkle in his eyes, "do you have the Yellow Leaf Number One? If not, I can help you get it. I have connections."

"I don't need any of that!" she said with sudden emotion. "All I need is love, some feelings beyond belief!"

It was clear to Spartacus that this Ofra girl was not very bright, since a smart woman sought more from a man than love. "You are definitely an Outlander!" he said, laughing as he took her hand in his.

"Spartacus, you have a beautiful name," Ofra said softly.

"It is a great name," he replied. "Have you ever heard of Spartacus, the leader of a slave rebellion in a faraway land? He was the bravest man of all ages. I was named after him, although there haven't been any slaves on this island for a long time, and I have nobody to liberate. However, a woman once told me that I was liberating women's hearts from excessive emotions."

Spartacus and Ofra spent the rest of the day together, walking, swimming in the Great Ocean, and dancing to the peculiar Vincentian music. Spartacus was attentive and affectionate, and Ofra was in heaven. She had yet to learn that Vincentian men regarded marriage as an anathema, and she fell madly in love with him.

It was late at night when Spartacus took Ofra to his stately mansion. For the first time, she realized how wealthy he was. There was marble on the walls, floors, and ceilings, and his home was full of antique furniture and paintings in heavy, gilded frames. In that magnificent setting, she gave him all her love and the passion burning within her. Ofra was ignorant of the fact that in no land would a man fall in love with a woman eager to stay with him on the first night.

Early the next morning, Spartacus left, asking her to come at dawn the next day to the tall tree with burgundy leaves.

Ofra's day dragged in anticipation of their reunion, and she arrived at the rendezvous hours before dawn. Spartacus showed up in a dark-blue shirt and black slacks, looking more handsome that ever, and swept her off feet. Hand in hand, they wandered the island's fragrant parks and cozy cobblestone streets, looking forward to another night of intense passion. She had no idea that for Spartacus, every night was nearly alike. He kept the doors of his heart locked securely from potential burglars.

In the morning, Spartacus made another date with Ofra, this time on a day that was a week away.

That week seemed like eternity to her, but when Ofra returned to the tree, Spartacus was nowhere to be seen. From that day on, a deep melancholy took hold of Ofra's heart. Her happiness was no more. Life on the island went on as before. People still went to work, ate, slept, and made love, but for Ofra, life had stopped.

She returned again to her favorite tree, but this time it was completely bare.

"Hello, tree, my dear old tree!" Ofra said. "Here I am again to keep you company. You must be as lonely as I am. I am very lonely indeed without him, my darling Spartacus. Who do you miss, tree? Your pretty burgundy dress, or perhaps the birds that nested on your branches but have now deserted you? Well, in your case, you'll soon get your pretty dress back, and the birds will return to sing their beautiful songs. As for Spartacus, he will never return to me. Like a migrating bird, he will fly farther and farther from me, warming up other nests as he goes, as far as his invisible wings can carry him."

The tree was silent. It didn't have answers to Ofra's questions, and the broken-hearted woman finally returned home.

A month flew by, and Ofra's favorite tree was again covered by lush burgundy leaves. When Ofra came to visit the tree, she saw Spartacus. She followed him with her longing stare as he walked down the path, unaware of the pair of loving, tear-filled eyes observing him from a distance. He was oblivious to the presence of the soul that yearned for him, the one who in all this time he had not missed even once. He was hurrying to meet another woman—a happy, trifling girl with red hair—leaving the shy and miserable Ofra far behind, her heart overflowing with love. He wrapped his hand around the waist of the one who loved him for his money, to whom he was just another sugar daddy.

Ofra watched Spartacus embrace the girl and then continue down the path. Ofra put her arms around the tree and leaned her head against its smooth, cool bark as she watched the chattering, frivolous woman put her arms around her Spartacus. Only a short distance separated them: the woman who's hand was wrapped around Spartacus's waist and the woman standing in the shade of the tree with burgundy leaves, squeezing its trunk ever tighter in her embrace.

"Why are you hugging the tree?" a female voice inquired. "Do you have no one else to hug?"

Ofra turned to see a young girl a long pink dress. She had long, dark, curly hair and beautiful green eyes.

"Don't cry over him," the girl said. "He won't love you."

Ofra brushed the tears from her cheeks and settled on the grass under the tree. The young girl sat beside her.

"Do you love him a lot?" the girl asked. Ofra burst into tears again. "Can you flirt with men, kid around with them?" the girl continued, unperturbed.

Ofra shook her head. "No, I cannot."

"Well, then, who can love you if you can't flirt with men?" the girl asked, looking surprised. "Did you see the redhead swoon when she saw that guy you're crying about? She could be faking it, you know. She knows how to charm a guy. Many men fall into that trap. Sometimes they fail to see genuine love but lose their heads from a well-planned loving game. In fact, I'm in the same predicament as you." The girl sighed. "The guy I love doesn't care for me either. See, I can't flirt or deceive; therefore, I'm doomed to suffer."

"Have you lived long on this island?" Ofra asked.

"As long as I can remember. See that big yellow house over there? That's where I live." The girl pointed to a large yellow building up on a hill with barred windows and a sign by the front door.

"Do you live with your parents?" Ofra inquired.

"No, I live with Desdemona. There's only two of us in the room," the girl said eagerly.

"With . . . Desdemona?" Ofra peered incredulously at the girl.

"Yeah. She fell in love with some Hamlet fellow and was about to escape with him to Denmark, but her husband, Othello, found out and began to strangle her when she was asleep. Now she lives with me, but eventually she'll travel to Denmark anyway 'cause she just can't imagine her life without Hamlet. I wish Othello loved me as much as he loved that woman. I wouldn't even think of looking at any Hamlets! No one would have loved him more than I did. Men are all alike, but women .

. . they're all different. I know that for a fact." She paused and gazed at the grass and then then looked up at Ofra. "Have you ever tried to write a letter to God?"

"God?" Ofra said. "Can one write a letter to . . . God?"

"Aha, there you are! See? Nobody does, right? People carry God in their hearts, think about Him, and beg Him for things, but no one, not one single person, actually writes Him a letter! Last night, for instance, when I was asleep, I was standing before Him. I asked Him some questions, and all He did was smile and say, 'That was meant to happen.' So, apparently, we're not to blame for our mistakes."

"I don't know," Ofra said sadly. "I've never thought about it."

"Last night when I was sleeping, I learned that God is pissed off at our island big time. He doesn't like our lifestyle. I want to give the people a warning before it's too late!" The girl rose to her feet and, without saying goodbye to Ofra, walked down the path, talking loudly to herself.

Hardly a week had passed since Ofra met the strange girl when a horrible calamity befell Vincent Island. Every Vincentian, male and female, who had kissed more than one man or a woman in his or her life fell terribly ill. Great chagrin fell over the land. The trees with multicolored leaves moaned, and the birds with brightly colored wings wept, but they were all helpless before God, and Vincent Island's population melted with each passing day. Frightening rumors spread over the island.

The dreadful affliction didn't spare Spartacus. He also fell victim to the disease, called the "Love Plague," since no man in the whole wide world could match Spartacus's lust.

Bent under the burden of her grief, Ofra went to see the love of her life. She found Spartacus in bed, alone and miserable. She kneeled by his bedside and took his head in her hands like the caring mother that he had long forgotten and a woman in love at the same time.

"Spartacus, my darling," Ofra said softly, stroking his hair.

"Please, don't touch me," Spartacus muttered weakly, although Ofra's warm touch felt extraordinarily good. "You could catch the disease"

"I won't be able to live without you anyway," Ofra whispered, kissing his red eyes and his swollen lips.

Spartacus was astonished to hear Ofra's words. Never before had he seen such powerful emotions. Then he remembered that he was doomed, and tears of self-pity streamed down his cheeks. "Where have you been all this time?" Spartacus murmured as he lay in Ofra's arms.

"I have always been close to you. You just never noticed. Even when you were wooing my redhead neighbor, promising her money, jewelry, and paradise on Earth, I was standing a short distance away from you under the tree with burgundy leaves, swallowing my bitter tears."

Those women! Spartacus thought. *They never miss a chance to rub it in, to remind us of all the offenses, big and small, that we have committed during our lives.*

"The redhead?" he said. "She died. She kissed lots of other men too."

"Did you love her, Spartacus?" Ofra asked, looking into his eyes with sadness.

"I . . . I guess I'm not really familiar with the feeling. I don't understand what it means . . . to love. When I met a woman, all I wanted was to touch her, kiss her, possess her, but after I'd had her, she ceased to exist for me. Tell me, what does it mean to love? The feeling you are talking about must exist on your island, but here on Vincent Island, it certainly doesn't."

"Tell me, Spartacus, do you love your money, your house, your land, and your jewelry?" Ofra asked.

"Oh, yes, of course. That kind of love I can understand. My money gave me freedom, independence. I bought lots of women with my money."

"You see, Spartacus, I love you the same way you love your money and then some," Ofra explained.

"Hmm . . . then you must love me very much indeed. Although I know for fact that no love is stronger than the one I feel for my money. Money always bought me what I desired, but now it has lost its power and become like the yellow leaves on the trees, abundant and useless." Spartacus gazed somberly at her. "Ofra, did you know I was fabulously rich? Women who didn't want me because of my dark skin color crawled on their knees for the houses, land, money, and jewelry that I gave them."

"Spartacus, my darling, I was never interested in your wealth. I would have loved you even if you had nothing but your yellow shirt with the dark-eyed bird on it, the symbol of your island! I won't leave you, Spartacus. I will stay with you till the end, and then together we will stand before God and beg Him not to separate us. You won't leave me anymore, Spartacus. You didn't want me in this life, so at least stay with me after death!" Ofra was on her knees before his bed, his head in her hands, looking into his eyes with a long, pleading stare.

"No, I won't leave you, Ofra," Spartacus whispered despondently. "No one wants me anymore."

"Oh, Spartacus, thank you, thank you for your kindness! I wish you could feel how much I love you! When I saw you with other women, heard you offer them yourself and your money, I went to church and pleaded with the Lord to rip you out of my heart, to help me forget you. But He didn't, and I am so grateful to Him now that you've agreed to stay with me after death."

"Are you for real, Ofra? I always thought money was the only thing that deserved such love! I thought all outlander women arriving to Vincent Island were after only one thing, Yellow Leaf Number One, and would stop at nothing to get it, that they would use all their charms to fool men like me!"

"Spartacus, you are much dearer to me than all the money in the world, more beautiful than all the yellow and burgundy leaves! You are more precious to me than my own miserable life! I praise the Lord for a chance to die together and be joined forever on the other side. I just wish you loved me in life!" Ofra bent down and kissed his pale, weakening hands. "Please tell me, darling, now that death is near, tell me that you love me too, just once before both of us are silenced for eternity!"

"Dear girl, I'm afraid I can't say it. I have never loved anyone. I beg you, tell me what I should feel!"

"Just say, 'Ofra, I love you as much as I love my money, my houses, and my land!'"

"But that can't be, Ofra. Never. Yes, I admit I liked you, but I also liked other women. Anyway, it doesn't make any difference now. I'm going to die soon. Why did you come to me, Ofra? Now you'll die too, and I haven't paid you for this. It's not right."

"Oh, dear Lord, Spartacus!" Ofra moaned, putting her arms around the dying man.

Ofra's happiness lasted for seven days. For seven days she stayed with Spartacus, confident for the first time that her lover wasn't going anywhere and that he would not steal away from his home in the morning after a steamy night.

On April 9, the seventh day, Ofra and Spartacus closed their eyes for the last time, never to open them again. The most handsome man on Vincent Island, lovely Spartacus—always happy, smiling, and proud of his wealth—lay side by side with Ofra, the sad woman who couldn't give up loving him. Her pale face still bore a soft smile, for she did, after all, keep her loved one for eternity, while her soul, together with his, soared to heaven, carrying their passionate plea to keep them together.

They were buried side by side in the shade of a tall tree with burgundy leaves, the leaves that never ceased to amaze her.

TOMORROW

When tomorrow comes, you will not be in it,
Vanished, gone as if never existed.
From the faraway lands words of love never reached,
To wake up your loved one from the distance.
Never warmed up her soul with such sweet, tender touch,
Never known to her, that she craved so much.

When tomorrow dawns, it will bring emptiness,
For you will not be there to fill it,
An impossible dream and a beautiful myth,
Dead is love that had never occurred.

Yet the heart will continue to beat as before,
Deep inside your dear image safekeeping,
Keep the love for you secret and won't tell a soul
How it yearns for your eyes, bitterly weeping.

When tomorrow comes, it will bury the dream
Of the love that was never forthcoming,
Fill the heart with solitude, make it forget
Sheer sweetness of love and a magic becoming.
It will teach heart a lesson to always recall
That in Heavens its fate was secured:
God his verdict returned - stay forever unloved,
Never warmed by love, that is assured.
He sentenced the heart to long years in the dark
Of the dungeon filled up with despair,
Make it weep day and night
With no hope of a flight,

And commiting its angst to the paper.

When tomorrow comes, it will bring misery,
For you will not be there to share it.
Days will pass without you
Heart will beat just for you,
And for you all eternity care.
Heart will keep very deep
Cherished image for ever
Warming up by the ambers of love's smothered fire.

When tomorrow comes, it will be like all days
Back when heart was of you not aware,
Aforetime when it felt not the bliss of your love,
When your closeness wasn't yet there.

Short affection of your unpredictable heart
Brought along unfamiliar contentment,
Then it took it away to remind poor heart:
Love's sojourn is prelude for resentment.

Love invades happy heart and it rips it apart,
Shedding blood and creating destruction,
Makes it moan with pain, again and again
Makes it pay for the bliss of seduction.

When tomorrow comes
Heart will vanish from Earth
Combusted by roaring blaze
As if fire of love that consumed it before
Hadn't finished its gruesome and merciless chore.

The wind will spread the ashes of cremated heart
Over Earth and oceans, far and wide,
Yet the pain of love spurned will not subside,
Since it stayed for so long deep inside.

Who will know how deep was heart's yearning for love,
Longing, craving, unable to deal with the fact
That it was never loved and rejected by ones
Who the heart was in love with so deeply.

FRIEND

A friend turned foe, the sweetness of fake passion
Dispersed and vanished like a weightless cloud.
And wounded heart, transfixed by such deception,
Cried out in pain and weeped out loud.

As if in days of yore it never suffered,
And never ached for anyone before,
He pledged his love with casual demeanor
And let the lonely heart to soak him up.

A friend turned foe, the mask slipped off the face,
By accident, with no intent, and there
Behind a handsome look and graceful poise,
Behold the trifle soul of hypocrite.
And bitter heart to Heavens turned for mercy.

What have I done to fall out of grace?
Do I deserve the misery and torment
You send my way consistently for years?
Do you believe I have no strength to beat?
But God was silent and the heart kept weeping
Without any tears, uninterrupted.

Why it absorbed the falsehood of the words,
The mawkish words he casually uttered?
Who made you think you'd feel the warmth of love
When you know better after years of trying?
Do you recall the anguish love did bring
While ripping you apart to little pieces?

Oh, yes, for starters, it had always been
A pleasant and caressing feeling
That brought you out from your loveless slumber,
Ignited fire, made you blaze with passion
Before into oblivion disappearing.

And every time the heart woke up in pieces,
Put them together, patching up the wounds,
Swore solemnly to never be again
Caught in the fatal web of sweet deception,
And ran away from love like from a leper.

Yet love would never leave the heart alone.
Time and again it would rekindle fire
And caught the poor heart in web of charming lies
To recommence the agonizing cycle.

Last love was short-lived,
The deception was by accident uncovered,
Gone was the falsehood of the empty words.
The lonely heart to solitude committed
To keep alive the lust for fake illusion
For once to be adored by the one
Who deep inside the scorching blaze restarted.

Is it too much to wish for someone's love?
Just once until the day when God
In Heaven confesses that He loved you
All the while!

Death

Death came to Earth
The earthlings run and hide
Unable to resist the Reaper's wrath.
Too long the people sought thy neighbor's death,
Too great was joy from seeing others' pain.
Too long the mankind was content to see
The broken hearts, maternal tears
Shed over bodies of the slaughtered children.

Death roams the Earth, seeks out those,
Who mulled the people under wheels of cars,
To see the look on their desperate faces
Before proceeding with the last embrace.

Grim Reaper enters in the homes of those
Who used to take the joy in others' pain,
To prove its point: there's no disparity in hearts
When one is burying his kin.

Death roams the Earth,
It reaps its deadly and impartial harvest
To make the people finally embrace
The angst of those who's hearts were scorched by fire
Beholding their loved for leisure slaughtered .

Death sores high above the Earth, its cold embrace
To all mankind unleashes somber warning:
This planet's all we have, there is no other place,
It looks like End of Days is finally dawning.

Death's grim design will come at gruesome cost,
To rip the life right off the face of planet,
So people understood what precious world they lost
And valued what they had as greatest tenet.

Death turned to be the Master of the Earth,
Which mankind squandered, year after year,
And blew it up, and flooded it with blood,
Without mercy, with abundant cheer.

Death came to Earth as penalty divine
For people not to forfeit their future,
To value life, feel mercy and compassion,
Not to rejoice in fellow humans' torture.

May Reaper's advent to our wicked world
Serve as a loud, frightening reminder:
Death's powerful and terrifying sword
Can devastate the World and leave no soul behind her.

BIRD IN CAGE

You thought I was a toy, you, cruel, heartless creatures,
Who gave you right to bury me alive?
Seek absolution for your sins in churches,
As you commit them right where you live and thrive.

You seek your fortunes and pursue your pleasure,
But I'm committed to your putrid cage,
You trimmed my wings and took away my treasure –
My freedom and the Sun's warm rays.

And now you wish for me to thrill your offspring
With pretty little tunes from dusk till dawn,
And give you joy by dumb and mindless twitting
All in exchange for view of your front lawn.

What of my joy, the one that you denied me,
Me, who with Liberty once flew?
You give me water that is dead and foul
To me, who's used to drinking morning dew.

The fodder that you shove into my feeder
Is bitter and repulsive prison slop.
I miss the taste of fresh cut grass on meadows
That's warmed up by the Sun's eternal love.

My tears roll down the bright and colored feathers,
The plumage that attracted you to me,
These tears come from aching heart of jailbird
Depraved of freedom and the godly glee.

I miss the sky that's peeking through your windows,
My soul still soars there among the clouds.
I beckon it with ruffle of my feathers,
But it will not descend from up above.

My heart and soul forever separated
The soul's up there, in the blissful sky,
The heart's in dungeon very deeply hated
So there's nothing left for me but cry.

And now, before the bell tolls final hour,
Until my heart has few remaining beats,
I want to do what's left within my power,
To bid my farewell to those I miss.

Farewell to Sun, I failed to reach your regions
To thank you for the warmth you amply shared.
Your rays can melt the steel and vaporize the stone,
But powerless they are my heart to warm.

Oh, endless Sky, my wings destined to fold
Beneath the blue abyss that used my wings to hold.
The empty space where Liberty resides,
And where I found happiness and pride.

Farewell to leaves on all the trees I knew,
I miss the days when in your crowns I grew.
I loved you all, and on depressing nights,
In my grave-cage this love was sole light.

Oh, how I wished to bust through hated walls
And sing again in God's celestial halls!
Farewell, my home shrub, once upon a time
You sheltered helpless fledgling that was I.

You were my roof on rainy, stormy nights,
You helped me up when I attempted flight.
Farewell to Freedom, you remain alone
In my home forest where shadows roam.

Where branches dreamed of little poets' songs,
And verses were composed all day long.
On somber days when skies were dark and foul
You had the company of my immortal soul.

So said the jailbird, and, all said and done,
It closed its eyes and was forever gone.
New day will dawn, another convict bird
Will make the cage its tight and gloomy world.

BLACK SEPTEMBER

In the dead of the night
The mother sheds her tears
Over a yellowed page of old newspaper
Featuring the picture of her son
Jumping to his doom
From the blazing tower.

Come again, my son, I will be waiting,
The mother utters and finally goes to bed.
Mommy, dear, don't cry, I couldn't perish
Without thinking of you,
The mother hears as she drifts to sleep.

My beloved son, let me know more.
Stumbling upon torn, charred bodies,
I wondered to the light and plunged,
Hoping something may stop the fall
And save my life for you, my dear mother.

On that distant, dreadful September day
I waited in the yard for you just like before
When you were late from school.
And then the paper came and there you were
You leaped from wicked flames
To lethal Death's embrace.

Forgive me, son, for failing to be there,
For trying not to wrestle you from Death!
Don't cry, dear mommy, didn't I hear you say
That men were mortal, all of men!

I may have said it, right,
But I could not portend
The fate of my beloved, little boy!
The little boy who had become a man.
On that day, mother, they sentenced me to Death,
Those monsters who were killing us
In name of their god!

My son, the God is one.
It was the people into monsters turned.
In Black September people shed their good
And Evil reigned, It creeped into our quiet home
And took my son, and buried me alive.

Don't cry, my dear mother lest your heart
Be pierced by another pain.
Dear son, my heart turned into stone that day,
Devoured by dark and bottomless abyss.

Pain dwells there all the time, there's no cure.
But, mother, I remember, every Spring
Your heart would blossom like an early flower
And fill with fragrance of the nature's youth!

My darling, the wind is howling
The Requiem for you who has been lost for good.
The mother says and grabs her heart
And cries from early morning to the night
Until the moment comes and in her dream
Her son is back alive.

COULD IT BE TRUE

My love, please, look into my eyes
Veiled by the sorrow's dark disguise
They lost the spark of former cheer
Since you abandoned me, my dear.

They keep the pain of love by you forgotten
Left for the dead, discarded and misused
Without you my life was truly rotten
My heart is bleeding, cut and badly bruised.

Could it be true that you returned from journey
Back by my side, the one I've ever craved,
And I can touch you every night and morning
Alone no more, no longer I'm depraved.

Alone no more on this gigantic planet,
With more people than water in the Ocean
Where lack of one means loss of all, I mean it
Without you the Sun won't rise again.

The flowers mourn: their beauty is unable
To enter vaulted chambers of my heart
For you alone I set my lavish table
No one to come and tear us apart.

From far away returned to me, my dear,
Perhaps, your heart could hear the distant call
Of other heart that needed you to steer
Your ship to shore where you can have it all.

Could it be that my heart will know the cheer,
Believe it can be blessed by love again?
Could it be that my sorrow's dark veneer
Fall from my eyes and take away the pain?

Are you aware what lonely heart could fancy
When flowers bloom and fragrance fills the air?
When Moon ascends to throne and stars are dancing
The loveless heart is filled with cold despair.

What's why on nights like these the Moon is hiding
Behind the cloud curtain in the skies
Afraid to see the tears the heart is crying
When tears in the eyes have dried.

CRYING ROSE

Rose cries when raindrops hammer
On its petals drumming ballads,
Wails the rose when mighty thunder
Splits the sky with lightning flashes.
Shakes the rose when winds of Autumn
Reap the leaves off fragile branches.

It was only days ago
That the Sun was fiercely blazing,
Now it hides behind the clouds,
Cares not that Death is looming
Over rose's shriveled petals.

Rose needs the warmth of Summer,
Yearns for solar hot embraces.
You, by hearts of many worshipped,
Know what of pain and torment?

Who your thorns remind of anguish
Of unanswered love forgotten?
Who inhaled your balmy fragrance
Wafting through the rose garden,
Waking up in tight embrace
Of the love that never happened?

Cry my rose, the Sun is worth it
Even when it fails to warm you,
In the midst of Autumn's ache.
But forget what Sun did promise
When it showered you with passion.
Failed to mention, time will come,
It will turn away as if it never
Caressed you.

It will calmly watch from heavens
How the ruthless wind attacks you,
Ripping off your festive garments
That for granted you have taken.
And your former dazzling beauty
Wind will carry 'cross the garden,
Smear with dirt so people know:
Death has no favorites.

In the death all mortals equal:
Somewhere in the nooks of garden
Shriveled petals slowly wither.
No one will believe, just yesterday
They shone with beauty.

Seasons change, the snow is mortal
And, behold, another rose
Springs to life in all its glory
At the very spot where now
You are weeping, unconsoled.

No one will ever know
How you feared the oblivion,
How you loathed the very notion
Of the farewell to the Sun.

Ruthless wind has no mercy
When it's ripping off your petals,
Spreads them wide, your pain dividing
For the Earth to suffer less.

Knows the wind without doubt:
Those petals were still breathing
And could last a little longer.
But the laws of fate are finite:
One that's doomed must pass away.

Cry, my rose, while rain is falling.
It comes to help when once
All tears have been shed.

CRY VIOLIN

Cry, violin, she's gone, she's gone for good,
From world beyond return she never would.
She'll never rush the time so hated snow
Yield to the bloom and sun's eternal glow.

Gone from face of Earth, not leaving slightest trace
For ground to intern. Extinct, erased.
Rejected by the Love, she won't be missed
Lost in the Heaven's glorious bliss.

Behold, the birds, she rises to the sky.
Don't try to catch her, she has gone too far,
Turned into distant, brightly twinkling star.

And tell the Wind - he is relieved from chore
Of drying tears this lonely soul did pour.
May lilacs no longer be ashamed
Of lover's absence, of the broken dates.

Of lover's failure to observe the blaze
That burned in her delighted, loving gaze.

To leaves and grass I say, don't fuss and moan
For someone who is now forever gone.
While dressing up in gold for Autumn's ball,
The one who loved you most, I prey, recall.

Who, under sun that no longer warmed,
Chased by the wind, beside you often soared
When Autumn storms, in their ferocious rage
The leaves and grass with cruel force engaged.

A lovely rose at dawn will shed its tears,
With not a soul around to quell its fears
That she will never smell its fragrant petals
With sadness in her heart that never settles

And hurts, for no one would take a duty
To liken her to rose's striking beauty.

No one will cry again when Autumn breeze
Will rip the rose apart in sad reprise,
No one to pick the petals strewn around
And bury them as treasure in the ground.

Oh, mighty Ocean, what is it you know
About the heart that lost its inner glow,
And turned to ashes to be washed away
By your high tide one miserable day?

The heart that blazed with love's eternal fire,
As hot and fiery as a funeral pyre,
To make you doubt that your awesome force
Is greatest of all elements on Earth.

Alas, the only force that put the fire out
Was one's cold heart, of this have no doubt.

So, prey, don't toss the burnt out heart around,
Don't batter it with waves, don't let it run aground.
The cruel life took care of abuse
And strangled love in greasy lyncher's noose.

Just take the ashes, scatter 'cross the waves
And memories commit to sandy graves.

Almighty Sun, she grew so tired to wait,
For your hot rays her heart to penetrate.
But you delayed, since you can't understand
The notion of mortality in men.

She was unhappy on the mortal Earth,
But what awaits her after her rebirth
When she departed cold and wretched world
To share your celestial abode?

DEATH OF STRANGER

The drifter was taken to the gallows…
The people were rejoicing everywhere,
But poor heart of mine was mourning
And, for an instant, our souls were one.

It was I, who stepped into the Chamber of Death,
Hands tied behind my back
To touch the fallen tear unable.

It was I, who had a scarf wrapped around my neck
To ease the pain of strangulation.

It was I, who was facing the loop of the rope,
My last window on the world I was leaving.

It was my eyes that were blindfolded
So that no one could see my tears.

It was my soul that was trembling,
Silently begging for mercy.

It was I who stepped on the trap door
And into the bottomless abyss,
The never-ending fall.

I knew with my mind that a felon
Was being brought to justice,
But my eyes refused to comply with reason,
Shedding tears for the loathesome creature.

Tonight he will rest in the grave.
Soggy soil as his mattress and pillow,
And a coffin lid as his blanket.

Tomorrow morning he will not awaken
For the first time in his miserable life.
Death will cure his ailments,
The pain will pass, left above the grave
Together with love, sorrow and doubts.

Tonight his soul will tremble
For the first time facing the ones he slaughtered.
His lifeless skin will shiver
At the sight of innumerable victims
Gathered to judge him.

Countless moans will fill the air,
Reverberating through the underworld
"Why did you torture and murder us?
For what greater purpose we suffered?"
The martyrs will cry out.

From this night on he will be condemned to solitude,
His universe shrunk to the space of the coffin.
Death will pardon his offences,
The grave will console him with peace,
And the Earth will be merciful too,
By not weighing too heavy on the diseased.

DON'T WEEP MY GUITAR

What do you weep about, my guitar?
Who left his soul behind inside you?
Who's heart is weeping in unison?
Perhaps, you weep for me…

He found me not and all my days
I spent without him and waited
When flowers bloomed on trees,
When rain did wash my tears away.

When yellow leaves were dying,
When snowflakes my solitude embraced.
Don't crucify me, torture, lie to me, guitar,
That I was sought and missed

When during sleepless nights in misery's embrace
I listened to the sweet talk of the stars
That ceased to be a dream and their twinkle
Would beckon me into another world
Where torment I'd forget.

Don't weep, guitar, I understand
That cup of misery I must drink up
As fate has ruled. The days of life will fade
And I will leave this world
That happiness denied to my tormented soul.

Who would surmise that solitude like noose
Was strangling my heart?
That heart of mine that loved
For good unloved remained?

But I will gain my peace
I knew not under Sun
When I will cross the line
And fade away.

Don't hurt that soul of mine, guitar,
The taste of love it has forgotten.
Don't strain your strings
To lift it up to Heaven.

And don't remind me that the Love
Remained a stranger to my tortured heart,
Remained a dream that never would come true ,
Afraid of fierce passion that was burning
Inside my lonely soul.

Don't weep, guitar, let me forget
That for this soul which yearned for Love
Yet Love knew not, the life has gone.

Weep, my guitar, cry tears but don't let
The Love forget that all my life
For Love I always longed,
That this was once the world
That I dwelt in!

DO YOU RECALL OLD MAN

Old man, do you recall her love for you those days?
And how you looked at her, dispassion in your gaze.
Back then when your young blood was boiling in your veins,
Your lips were cold as ice when they would touch her face.

You thought the youth would last into infinitude
You frolicked with the tramps and stayed away from prudes.
Once on a fine Spring day you turned and walked away
From one and only love who wanted you to stay.
She spoke to moon and stars on sleepless, lonely nights,
While she was loving you, she was dying slowly.

Old man, remember passion in your eyes?
Before the old age doused the fire inside.
Those days are gone, extinguished is the fire,

Decrepitude succeeded the desire.
Far off from you, she relished their glare,
Consumed by anguish, ravished by despair.
Her own eyes' sorrowful abyss
Away from her you hardly ever missed.

Old man, do you recall how time and time again
You uttered words of love without slightest strain?
You sang the songs of love to those who never cared,
Not to the one who thought of you as dream that never came through.

The one who's heart for you kept on for years yearning,
And on who's skin your touch continued burning.
Depraved of your embrace you generously granted
To scores of groupies by your charm enchanted,
Her loving heart was weeping day and night.
But you were deaf to heart's incessant wailing,
Consumed by your pursuit of butterflies' free flight.

Old man, how would you like to learn about being
Without the one for whom your heart is dreaming?
The Sun destroys the grass and dries the streams,
　Only the heart wouldn't let the Sun close by,
　　It misses you, so distant and so dear.
　You - happy, careless, who stole its joy of life.

　Depraved of love and, thus, depraved of light,
　　The heart is wailing on a lonely night,
For one who found bliss in others' sweet embrace,
　　The one locked the heart in gloomy maze.

　Old man, life's Summer season doesn't last:
　　Before you know it, happiness is past.
Eyes' sparkle's gone and blood is running slow,
　The heart is crushed by fortune's mighty blow.
　　The pain of love rejected never leaves it,
　　It weeps because no one has ever loved it,
　　　Another heart was chosen instead.

DRIFTER

The fog descended upon Earth
Soaked up compassion for the poor heart
And with compassion he did take in passion
Wild passion that had promise of the bliss

And radiated joy. It called itself the Love.
Bewitched the poor heart, seduced with paradise.
And in the end it fought the futile fight
With musty apathy

And soon, the battle lost, it caved in to defeat
And drowned the heart in ocean of despair.
The fog descended upon Earth,
It kept the loyalty to heart
Just for one sigh of bliss that it provoked.

And grateful, it deprived the heart of cheerless love.
The wind embraced the trees and branches broke
In tribute to departed love,
The gentle leaves all shook in fright and feared for life.

In fog's tight embrace the Love did contemplate:
Was I so foolish to depart from heart I settled in for good?
The fog ascended high with Love in arms
And stars in heaven moved aside in awe.
Love recognized them as its kin and, behold,
It shone as fiercely as the brightest star.

Abandoned on the Earth, the Love
In heaven did become a shining star
That shines upon all lovers in this World
Who seek its warmth and light eternally.

Deprived of Love, the heart resented life,
It cried the bitter tears for its loss:
Where have you gone, my Love,
The one that dwelt inside for so long,
The one that shadowed the Sun and opened path to Moon,
The one that poisoned me by sweet and throbbing pain?

You preached eternity, and yet you slipped away,
Unable to forgive a harmless little sham!
Red leaves of fall, who's crimson shroud
Is envied by the green leaves of the Spring,
Ask mighty wind why blows it off the candle of our love,
And where it takes our dreams.
So screamed the heart in misery and pain.

FLOWERS

What are you sad about, dear flowers,
What bothers you in midst of breezy Summer day?
Aren't you excited to perceive the beauty
Of lovely petals confetti that whirl
In playful hands of Summer wind?

T'was just yesterday when you were
Admiring yourselves and shone with bliss
Under the warm Spring Sun.
You knew not of the life's short span on Earth,

You knew not that the beauty full of vigor
Is even shorter! Oh, dear flowers,
That traveler who longs the journey past
Can she be lonely amongst the throngs of people
On this Earth?

Or could it be, perhaps, that Love's exuberant Bloom
has withered in her lover's soul, just like You have?
Or could it be that she mourns her
Life's dream she buried on this day?

Perhaps, she realized that once she fell on Earth
Just like the flowers' bloom, she lost the fame of yore?
Her love still sores in the sky: akin a bird untamed
Who's destiny is sealed.

Afflicted by the love and never loved, how strange!
Woe to the heart that's destined love to keep:
Its bleeding soon won't stop!

The breeze now beckons, carrying the petals
Away. And traveler grabs them
In honor of the love long dead,
And mourns the fate which nailed her
To the eternal cross of solitude.

FOG

The fog descended upon Earth
Soaked up compassion for the poor heart
And with compassion he did take in passion
Wild passion that had promise of the bliss

And radiated joy. It called itself the Love.
Bewitched the poor heart, seduced with paradise.
And in the end it fought the futile fight
With musty apathy

And soon, the battle lost, it caved in to defeat
And drowned the heart in ocean of despair.
The fog descended upon Earth,
It kept the loyalty to heart
Just for one sigh of bliss that it provoked.

And grateful, it deprived the heart of cheerless love.
The wind embraced the trees and branches broke
In tribute to departed love,
The gentle leaves all shook in fright and feared for life.

In fog's tight embrace the Love did contemplate:
Was I so foolish to depart from heart I settled in for good?
The fog ascended high with Love in arms
And stars in heaven moved aside in awe.
Love recognized them as its kin and, behold,
It shone as fiercely as the brightest star.

Abandoned on the Earth, the Love
In heaven did become a shining star
That shines upon all lovers in this World
Who seek its warmth and light eternally.

Deprived of Love, the heart resented life,
It cried the bitter tears for its loss:
Where have you gone, my Love,
The one that dwelt inside for so long,
The one that shadowed the Sun and opened path to Moon,
The one that poisoned me by sweet and throbbing pain?

You preached eternity, and yet you slipped away,
Unable to forgive a harmless little sham!
Red leaves of fall, who's crimson shroud
Is envied by the green leaves of the Spring,
Ask mighty wind why blows it off the candle of our love,
And where it takes our dreams.
So screamed the heart in misery and pain.

GEESE FLYING SOUTH

The geese are leaving, southbound,
The heart is aching, full of grief,
Perhaps, at their destination
They'll see the one it's aching for.

A part of heart will stay forever
In those warm and distant regions,
The one part that forestalled its warming
In those lands by sun endowed,
The envy of the northern realm.

Ahead of time the leaves have sprouted,
Brighter than before,
With lilacs' scent, with tenderness of rose
Another heart slipped in without a warning.

It was forgotten, but heart still sadly gazes
At skies above that carry geese formations
Proceeding south, certain in belief
That southern sun will warm them up with love,
Unknowing that the sun can't warm the heart
Another heart had ruthlessly rejected.

The geese are flying off to distant lands,
By winter chill intimidated, unaware
Of heart's heartache by other heart forgotten,
Which has been frozen since that fateful spring.

By other hearts for many years worshipped,
It was rejected by the only one
That found the way into its very core.

That spring day when the wind was chasing rose petals
And filled the heart with blissfulness of magic
Turned out to become the day of grief,
The onset of the suffering to come.

The wind subsided, hiding from the question:
Why rose's fragrance brings the pain of loss?
Why rip off petals of the rose in bloom like
Ripping heart from lover's open chest?

In vain the sun was knocking on heart's door,
It couldn't find the bliss in solitude.
In those lands where sun is shining brighter,
The birds wake up before the dawn starts breaking
To see the tears of those who are abandoned,
Who's love was deemed to other heart's rejection.
From those tears comes the inspiration
Picked up by birds to make up their songs
And spread around the world with own refrain.

Oh, how much pain pours from the eyes of those
Who spend the sleepless nights in their backyards
And gaze at stars.
That's why a human heart does skip a beat
When birds begin to sing the song of love,
The very love that lights one heart on fire
And make the other one to flee in panic.

From distant lands where sun abounds,
Where geese are flying to partake of warmth,
She ran away long time ago, having left
Her heart behind to stay unloved forever.

The wind continues harvesting the petals
Of roses blooming in the summer gardens.
It brings those petals to rejected hearts
To breathe a little love in their lifeless shells
And swiftly runs away, avoiding capture
And answers to inevitable queries:
Where does it take the love for many years awaited?
What makes the love to fly away with wind,
Abandoning the heart to mourn its loss for years?

The geese are flying off to southern lands,
Their happy quacking makes the world aware
That southern sun will warm them up with love,
Oblivious to melancholy that reins in lonely hearts
Of those left behind, who's love was taken
Away by ruthless wind.

IF I FAIL TO SAY

If I fail to say it when Death comes calling,
Please, tell the Wind I loved him all life long.
I will not grudge him that he failed
To blow all pain off my immortal soul.
And tell him not be jealous of the ocean:
I split my heart in half between the two!

And let him know that the smell of grass
He used to bring from distant fragrant fields
My heart filled with chagrin and longing
For far-off days of youth when I was loved!

Please, tell the Life, which granted minute bliss
That I kept cherishing the meager days of Spring!
When lavish flowers that reached fool bloom
Their petals dropped to yield to nascent ones,
I couldn't stop laughing at myself.

Please, don't forget to tell the Love
That I hold no grudge for tearing my heart apart.
I had but one admirer on this Earth:
A faithful and doting companion,
An aide-de-camp, whose name is Solitude.

I hold no rancor for the Sleepless Nights
That kept their vigil at my lonely bedside.
When I cross over to the other side,
I'll drown in peace like in the deep of Ocean.

Yet my naïveté amused the Ocean,
Who raised his mighty waves to touch the sky
And flogged the beach without any mercy,
The same beach where I used to muse of peace.

The rain weeps gently, bidding farewell
To Summer's lazy days.
The fallen leaves are whispering to me
The song of true and everlasting Love
That passed me by without looking back.

A flock of birds takes off for distant lands
Their freedom-loving spirit trails along
Oblivious to those who are trapped
Within the walls of suffocating stone.

A herd of clouds drifts above my head
Beneath sapphire skies they play with wind
And flaunt their hazy, handsome robes.
They hurry not, eternity awaits.
They'll never understand the wretched one
Who's days are numbered.

The withered leaves take flight and fall on Earth
Just like my days that fly into abyss
From which there's no return
And where Time itself is doomed.

LAST DROP OF RAIN

In flower garden, at the height of bloom
A maiden's weeping on a rainy noon.
Deprived of love and gasping for the air,
    Her face distorted by a listless stare.

Rain mixed with tears streaming down her cheeks,
    It is aware of the ancient trick:
The time will heal the heartache, sooth the pain,
    Allowing the heart to love again.

Competing with the rain the maiden weeps,
    And heavens' help she feverishly seeks:
May thunder roll and wake the dormant heart,
Which wrecked her life and tore her soul apart.

On scalding noon the rain keeps falling down,
It washes tears of pain from face that frowns
    The very face that shared its lovely grace
With flowers that adorn this charming place.

She's so young, she has a lot to learn
About love that pure hearts does burn.
So often, as we give our lovers more,
We tempt them our feelings to ignore.
And as we strive to melt their icy hearts,
    We're drifting ever far and far apart.

She's young and pure, she is yet to learn
For many more with years she will yearn.
And many times the tears' tangled lace
The rain will wash off her delightful face.

The rain is weeping on this Summer noon
It knows: life will play a finite tune.
The smile will perish in our maiden's eyes,
Gray hair will tell of years' mournful prize.

The maiden knows not that time and time again
She'll die of love in ever pouring rain.
Abandoned and unloved she'll shed her tears
Lamenting all the wasted golden years.

Too young to know that in vain she'll wait
For his embrace at night, on starry date.
And on the sand of golden ocean shore
The words of love she'll hear no more.

Until the last and fateful drop of rain
To wash away the tear's stinging stain,
She will embrace the loneliness and pain
And never dwell in lover's arms again.

LEAVES

Leaves are mourning golden color
Fall has painted their girlfriends,
They are mourning when it's raining,
When the wind is thrashing branches,
Able not to find its peace.

Know leaves that on such dark day
Death may come like bolt of thunder,
Claiming its forsaken victims
That will fall like knights in battle
Ripped off branches by the wind,
And destroyed without mercy
In some crazy, wild vendetta.

Sun will shine, as always, brightly,
Rain will fall to feed the grasses,
And amongst the early blossoms
Birds will chant the hymns to Spring
That will fill with great contentment
Lonely hearts that ache for passion.

Everything will be like always,
But today the leaves will wither
No miracle will save them.
Sun won't shine for them tomorrow,
Bare trees will soon forget them,
They will turn to worthless garbage,
Useless litter on the ground
That in plastic bags will rot.

But the leaves don't want to wither,
Know leaves that Winter's snows
Won't arrive until December,
And it's not their time to die.

True, the Sun will shine tomorrow
And the Spring will bring new sprouts,
But the Sun can't love the newbies
Like it loved the old cohort.

But the wind keeps thrashing branches
That are shedding yellow soldiers
Battle-weary in the struggle
For their miserable lives.

Wind is soulless, it can't fathom
What it means to leave existence.
Knows wind that death may happen
Any hour, any minute,
Pretty daydreams interrupting,
It will end the joy of life.

Time will come and their children
Will be basking in the Spring Sun,
Just as if their rotting parents
Never rustled on the branches,
And the Sun didn't warm their skin.

But on this gray Autumn morning
Leaves fall down from the branches
Making space for new arrivals
That will come to be next Spring.

They are tumbling, spinning slowly
T'wards the ground where death is waiting
Under same sky where for some time
They were rustling blissfully.

Morrow'll bring abundant sunshine,
But the leaves won't feel its warmness:
They'll be raked and neatly packaged
For the fire to devour them.

Rain keeps weeping for the victims
That this world abandoned early,
Leaves are sobbing, falling slowly
In the puddles of bitter tears…

This will happen on the morrow,
When the rain its thirst will quench,
Not today, when leaves are destined
Their early grave to meet.

MUSIC

The Spring arrived when everyone quit waiting,
But leaves are not in rush to sprout, hesitating,
They fail to comprehend impatience of the branches
That waited for so long oppressed by weight of snow.
The lovesick fog hangs out in the brush and hugs the trees,
Its love absorbed the Spring, obscured the way,

So nervous birds abandoned their prey
And lost the way to nests that held new life,
They joined the chorus of exited peers
In their plea to fog to ease their fears
And leave the hospitable woods
Where hungry offspring begged for food.

The rain came pouring from the cloudy sky:
The bliss of Spring made poor fellow cry.
The wind pried out of fair maiden's hands
A flower which she used with no pretense
For fortune-telling purpose to inquire
If her Prince Charming had the same desire.

The flower with its remaining petal
Preserved the secret of her lover's heart:
He loved her not and they would drift apart.
The bubbling brook took over from the wind
And carried wretched flower with its secret
Of love that never meant to be.

The music plays a cheerless sound
Ignoring gorgeous Spring around,
The flowers don't smell and fell to ruin
The altar where love once reigned.
Worshipped in vain by the young and old
It was but lie by priests sold.

An orange bird on branch up there
Cries with the tune that harts does tear.
The leaves are pleading with the wind
To shake off tears of their skins.
They know not the reason why
In Spring someone would need to cry.
In their week-long, blissful lives
They knew no misery or strife.

Poor leaves assume that bliss is norm
Until they weather mighty storm
And get a whipping by the hail
And feel like heart that's doomed to fail
Destroyed by cruel, spiteful love,
Like hail descending from above.

The tiny leaves on branches sway
Touched gently by the silver wind
To whom they pledged eternal love
But Fall will come and from above
The wind with vengeance will descend
And to their doom the leaves will send.

The music plays its mournful score,
The joy of Spring to be no more,
Reminds the trees: you now bloom
But very soon you'll meet your doom.
For nothing's lasting on this Earth
Except its own stone and dust.

Yet, branches fail to yield to gloom
With leaves that soon will meet their doom,
With slayer wind that harbors death.
They waltz to someone's anguished tune.
Their older kin that rots in soil
Not far from carnival's tinfoil
Aware fully that demise
Is what once was their paradise.

They know the pain, but yearn for Spring
When up on branches birds did sing
And leaves would flutter in the breeze
Convinced that life will never cease.

The tune bemoans the love long lost
That heart would not recall to host.
Presiding on the wake for love
Betrayal stares from above
While poor heart still weeps and mourns
By treason wounded, badly burnt.

Oh, music, why continue play?
Why paint Spring days in black and gray?
As green young leave in height of Spring
I joined this World of love to sing.
I sacrificed my heart and soul
On love's altar like Sun to burn.

And though the Sun did brightly glare
Its shine had none of warmth to share,
And when its rays would touch my soul
They burned like hot and blazing coals.

My heart's joy was a brief affair:
Pierced by apathy's glum stare
It withered like a new spring leaf
That learned the spring storm's brutal grief.

I was desired, haunted and adored
By those about whom I never cared,
But objects of my own desire
Would never light their hearts on fire.
Thus whispered fair maiden, chasing after
The flower that was carried by the stream.

And music plays on, cries of love
That longed to be Eternal Spring,
But never lasted through the Winter.
Destroyed by Treason, she is mourned
By sad strings' tune and dismal song
On Spring's May day when Earth delights
And basks in Sun's eternal light.

REMEMBER ME, O LORD

Remember me, O Lord,
When I ascend to thy heavenly kingdom,
The kingdom of love and peace.
Remember the one who suffered
Great misery on this Earth.

I longed for love like I longed for thee
Who looked down at my grief
With disbelief and contempt.
I was content with meager bits of bliss
Thou sent my way so I can bear
The burden of my wretched life.

I sought love like a busy bee
Seeks flower all bright and fresh,
Eager to fill my home
With fragrance and with joy
Of budding love.

It warmed my soul in chilliness of night,
But only to deliver
Another ruthless blow
And cast me into the abyss of pain.

My heart was pierced by the merciless thorns,
Love flower's generous gifts.
Blood oozed from jagged wounds
And fragile petals soaked.

I am a soldier on the battlefield of love
Exhausted and all bloodied by the fight
Yet always living through the hell of battle
And craving for one more.

Remember me, O Lord, this is I
Who sought deceptive sweetness of Love
Like wretched pilgrim seeks a blessed well
Amidst scorched desert under glaring Sun.

I longed to taste love potion sweet and fresh
To quench thirst on my eternal quest.
Alas, it was for naught.

Remember me, O Lord,
When I ascend to thy heavenly kingdom,
The kingdom of love and repose.
Remember the one who found
None of this on thy Earth.

SHAKESPEARE'S SONETS

When I complete my tenure on this Earth
My final wish will be to pack along your sonnets.
In them the pain and angst of tortured soul of mine.

Oh, William Shakespeare, what price you paid
For verse eternity, what pain you bore!
I know, I've been there.

Behind thick foliants how many people gleamed
The anguish of your soul by treason wounded?
You walked the path of suffering and sorrow
Towards the gleaming tower of greatness!

Your golden stylus in eternity emblazoned
The one who was a naught without you.

Although there are centuries between us
I still can hear in the silent night
The martyr's moans, a soul just like mine.

You are the great Shakespeare, no doubt.
And me, I'm just a speck of dust, a tiny droplet,
But your sonnets you must have, truly, copied
from my tormented soul.

By whim of destiny depraved of peace and love
My poor heart is weeping year round
Awash in misery...

The withered foliage – another grim reminder
Of my impending fate which reeks of soggy earth
Soon to embrace the one
Who dwelled, not lived in this eternal world
In search of happiness.

Oh, William Shakespeare, so distant, yet so close!
You, of all people, have discovered
Unanswered love's cruelty and anguish!

I follow behind you in your footsteps
Still, after all this time
The same I carry burden
And wondering if posterity would record
The screams of martyr.

UNCLE TOM'S CABIN

The days of my far-away childhood
When I wept over "Uncle Tom's Cabin"
Have returned and swept me away.

Though I came to this World
As a fair-skinned one,
Always thought of the black ones
As brothers of mine.

When the merciless whip
Was tainting white cotton
With the red blood of blacks
My heart was weeping.

From the tears of mothers
Who's children were sold on the block,
From the suff'ring of those
Who toiled in the fields dawn to dusk
A majestic tree has arisen.

Fertilized by the ashes of slaves,
Irrigated by blood of the blacks,
Stood the tree as if spiting the ones
Who its branches did cut.
And it sprouted the roots deeper still.

It was yearning for freedom and Sun
And, behold, many branches were lost
But it reached for the dream and success
And ensured its right to exist
As an equal among the peers.

So, that day, when the Dream of all blacks
On the wings of the Hope
Flew into the greats halls of the main
Edifice of the land,

Like in days of my past
Over pages of "Uncle Tom's Cabin"
I was weeping my heart out
Still feeling the pain of the past.

1. BRITISH MARINE ENGINER
2. THE WITCH
3. SLEEPLESS NIGHTS
4. LETTERS
5. THE VINCENT ISLAND
6. TOMORROW
7. FRIEND
8. DEATH
9. BIRD IN CAGE
10. BLACK SEPTEMBER
11. COULD IT BE TRUE
12. CRYING ROSE
13. CRY VIOLIN
14. DEATH OF STRANGER
15. DON'T WEEP MY GUITAR
16. DO YOU RECALL OLD MAN
17. DRIFTER
18. FLOWERS
19. FOG
20. GREESE FLYING SOUTH
21. IF I FAIL TO SAY
22. LAST DROP OF RAIN
23. LEAVES
24. MUSIC
25. REMEMBER ME O LORD
26. SHAKESPEARE'S SONETS
27. UNCLE TOM'S CABIN

Translated from Russian by Anatol Kardiukov

www.ingramcontent.com/pod-product-compliance
Lightning Source LLC
LaVergne TN
LVHW091553060526
838200LV00036B/814